When his golden retriever Rochester discovers a body during one of their nightly walks, reformed computer hacker Steve Levitan must look to his neighbors for suspects. Could a killer be lurking along the oak-lined streets? Steve inherited his townhome from his father, and it's more than just a house to him—it's the place where he recovered from the loss of two miscarried babies, the pain of losing his parents and the misery of his brief incarceration. Now that he has a new sweetheart, and a loving dog, protecting his home is even more important.

Could someone in the homeowner's association be sabotaging efforts to keep River Bend a well-maintained place to live? It's up to Steve and Rochester to dig up the clues to bring a murderer to justice, and protect the place they call home.

Mr. Plakcy did a terrific job in this cozy mystery. He had a smooth writing style that kept the story flowing evenly. The dialogue and descriptions were right on target.

-Red Adept

Steve and Rochester become quite a team and Neil Plakcy is the kind of writer that I want to tell me this story. It's a fun read which will keep you turning pages very quickly.

-Amos Lassen – Amazon top 100 reviewer

In Dog We Trust is a very well-crafted mystery that kept me guessing up until Steve figured out where things were going.

-E-book addict reviews

Neil Plakcy's Kingdom of Dog is supposed to be about the former computer hacker, now college professor, Steve Levitan, but it is his golden retriever Rochester who is the real amateur sleuth in this delightful academic mystery. This is no talking dog book, though. Rochester doesn't need anything more than his wagging tail and doggy smile to win over readers and help solve crimes. I absolutely fell in love with this brilliant dog who digs up clues and points the silly humans towards the evidence.

– Christine Kling, author of Circle of Bones

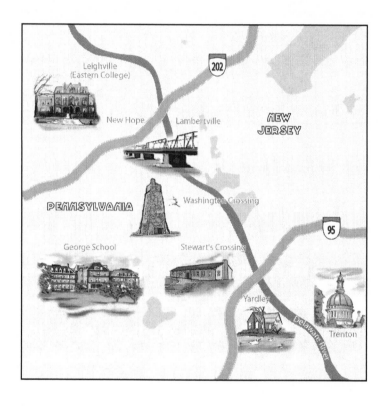

Dog's Green Earth
A Golden Retriever Mystery

Neil S. Plakcy

Samwise Books
www.mahubooks.com

1: Fine Management

"If these jerks at the homeowner's association think they're going to force me to take down the name plate above the garage, they're barking at the wrong squirrel," I said.

My golden retriever, Rochester, rose from his place on the kitchen floor and came over to me, responding either to the agitation in my voice – or the word "squirrel." I sat on one of the white wooden chairs around the kitchen table and rubbed his head.

"That's an interesting mixed metaphor," Lili said. "Can you translate that into standard English, please?" Lili was my significant other, a fiery, beautiful, dark-haired descendant of Polish Jews who had transited through Cuba before coming to the United States. I was lucky to have fallen in love with her a few years before and even luckier that, after a year's courtship, she had moved in with me and Rochester.

Usually I was the picky one when it came to grammar – I had a master's in English, after all, and had been an adjunct professor of English off and on at Eastern College, where I got my undergraduate degree, and where I currently managed a conference center for the college. Lili was a photojournalist who chaired the Fine Arts department and was accustomed to expressing herself through the lens of her camera.

"This letter," I said, and I handed it to her.

The name plate in question was one that my father and I had

made together, when I was about ten years old. He was an engineer and a skilled craftsman, and he had a wood shop in the basement of our house, with a long workbench and racks of obscure tools.

I was not so handy, but I loved my dad, and when he suggested we make something together I was all in. He sketched out our last name, Levitan, as if written by an architect, in clear and precise lettering. As I watched, he traced the letters over a piece of beautiful light-brown hickory wood.

Then he turned on a blowtorch and handed it to me. The handle of the torch was warm against my palm, the scent of the propane gas an assault on my nostrils. But I knew that I was safe with my father beside me.

He guided my hand as we etched the letter L into the wood. I was a little shaky, so after that he did the burning while I watched. Then I applied coat after coat of lacquer over the wood at his direction.

When were all finished, he drilled a hole in each side of the plaque and climbed up the ladder to hang it over our garage. After my mother died and he sold the house, he brought the sign with him to the townhouse in River Bend and hung it over the garage once more.

While he adjusted to life as a widower, I was going through my own trouble in California. My marriage was falling apart, ending in divorce while I spent a year in state prison for computer hacking. My father died while I was still incarcerated, and after I was released on parole I moved back to Bucks County and into his townhouse.

I remembered pulling up in the driveway after my flight back to Pennsylvania. Seeing that plate above the garage told me that even though I had no job, no relationship, and a criminal record, I'd come home.

I looked over at Lili as she scanned the letter the association had sent, demanding I take the sign down because it did not conform to the design criteria in the by-laws, which preached against handmade exterior décor and wanted to keep us to a kind of Stepford-like uniformity. If I didn't comply, I'd be fined.

"Their concern seems over the top," Lili said about the letter. "I'll bet it's because of this new software. I read about it on *Hi Neighbor*."

Lili had joined that online community of IRL (in real life) neighbors, where they shared notices of lost cats and recommendations on plumbers and handymen. People posted information on crime and vandalism in neighboring areas, though we were lucky that our gates and twenty-four-hour security kept us fairly crime-free.

Lately, the communications had all been complaints about the way River Bend was being managed. She pulled her laptop over and showed me the way the site was organized, and all the maintenance complaints that had been posted by residents of River Bend.

I hadn't paid much attention to the things that were mentioned there, though I did get irritated when Rochester looked like he was walking through a field of young corn as the grass reached up and tickled his flanks, and I had to push the stalks around to get down to whatever poop he had left.

I pointed to one of the complaints. "This is that software you mentioned, right?"

Even though I'd had to give up my computer career as part of my parole, I was still interested in anything innovative—especially if it affected my life.

"It's called a fine management program," Lili said. "Pennsylvania Properties bought it a couple of months ago, and they're rolling it out at all the homeowner's associations."

River Bend was a gated community, and we had contracted with Pennsylvania Properties to take care of the property. Todd Chatzky, a young guy with heavily greased dark hair, was our on-site manager, with a middle-aged woman named Lois as his secretary.

Todd had been working at River Bend for a couple of years by then, and I recalled the first time I met him, when the association sponsored a barbecue to welcome him. He spoke briefly about his background—that he had served in the Army in Iraq, when he had seen first-hand how important community was. He drove interpreters into small towns and loved the way everyone knew each other and looked out for each other. "That's the kind of management I'd like to bring to River Bend," he said.

Things had started out well. Todd renovated and expanded the clubhouse to include more space for neighborhood groups, and brought in yoga teachers, meditation leaders, and real estate brokers who talked about maintaining value in our property.

Rochester got tired of being petted, and he sprawled on the floor in front of me. I sat back and tried to remember how things had been at River Bend back then.

The board had been pretty hands-off, leaving everything up to Todd. Then there had been an incident with the landscaping crew, where they cut down a big branch which fell on Earl Garner's Mercedes SUV. He was unhappy at how long it took to get reimbursed for the damage, and he used that, and a few other small things, to lead a coup that took over the association board of directors.

Garner had made no bones about his desire to get Todd fired. But his bosses at Pennsylvania Properties backed him up, and he and the board entered into an uneasy truce. I was sure that many of the problems going on in River Bend were a result of that lack of desire to work together. I wondered if this new software was a cooperative venture between the board and Pennsylvania Properties, or another point of dissent between them.

"What does this fine management program do?" I asked Lili.

She looked up from her phone, where she had been reading something. "Todd hired a kid to ride around in a golf cart and document homeowner violations with photographs. Then Todd reviews the photographs and decides which houses are violating the terms and conditions in the homeowner's agreement. He uses the software to generate letters to the homeowners and track when they pay their fines. If they don't pay, they get an escalating series of letters, and the fine goes up with time."

"That's awful."

"It certainly is if you get one of these letters," Lili said, handing it back to me. "One of the women on Hi Neighbor is facing a thousand-dollar fine because the stucco trim on her townhouse is dirty. She's barely scraping by on Social Security and she can't hire one of those companies to come in and clean it, and she's been begging and pleading Todd for an exemption, but he just ignores her."

"I see Todd riding around on his golf cart sometimes when I'm walking Rochester. He used to be such a friendly guy, but now I wave hello and he pretends not to see me."

"There's a movement on Hi Neighbor to get rid of him," Lili said. "People say that it's his job to enforce all the community rules, not just the ones from the design committee. That he's not strong enough to stand up to the board, and we need somebody who can rein them in. I can show you the messages if you want. And we should post something there about how ridiculous this demand is."

"Does that do any good?"

"If we can get enough people to complain about Todd to Pennsylvania Properties then maybe they'll convince him to stand up to the board, or replace him with someone who can."

"How do you know the problem is with the board? Maybe Todd's just gotten lazy, or he's overwhelmed with the work."

"Steve. You've lived in this house for six years and you have never paid attention to anything that the board does. From what I read on Hi Neighbor, most of the board members own multiple properties and rent them out. They're only interested in what benefits them. If you want to see some changes, you should run for the board."

"Me?"

"Well, I can't, because I'm not a homeowner."

Though Lili had moved in with me nearly three years before, we were not married, and I had not changed the deed to add her name to it. We had written wills the year before, leaving our estates to each other, and we'd both agreed that protected her enough. Neither of us had assets that pushed us over the limits for tax-free inheritance, and we both had been scarred by previous marriages and divorces. We weren't eager to rush into anything that involved licenses and rings.

"I don't think I'd have the patience to be on the board," I said. "Though I am going to the fine committee meeting to complain."

"Good luck with that," Lili said. "Nobody on Hi Neighbor has gotten any positive resolution that way."

"The committee hasn't dealt with me yet," I said, as Rochester sat up and nuzzled me.

§§§§

I was so irritated with the letter from the association that I couldn't focus on anything, so I grabbed Rochester's leash and took him out for a walk. It was early evening and the sun was setting, bouncing golden shards off the west-facing fanlight windows and the gray-roofed pergolas atop certain models.

Rochester stopped periodically to sniff and pee as we walked up Sarajevo Court—all the streets in River Bend are named for Eastern European cities. When we turned the corner onto Minsk Lane, I was reminded once again of the irony that my grandparents and great-grandparents had struggled to escape Eastern Europe, only to have me end up walking past street signs that would have read better in the Cyrillic alphabet.

Eric Hoenigman, one of our neighbors, approached, walking

his big white English setter Gargamel, named by his son after the Smurf villain. Gargamel was even taller than Rochester, though his frame was all muscle, and he had a freckled red head.

Eric unhooked Gargamel's leash, and big setter came rushing over. Rochester went down on his front paws in the classic play position, and I unclipped his leash, too. The two of them chased each other in and out of yards and around hedges as Eric and I watched with amusement.

"Now if they could just manage to toss a ball back and forth between each other we've have a perfect play date," he said, nodding down the street, where a man in a sport wheelchair was tossing a ball to a young boy, rolling back and forth to catch it in return. I'd seen the man on occasion, but didn't know him by name.

Watching them play, I felt a momentary pang of lost fatherhood. After I finished my MA in English at Columbia, I was sharing an apartment in New York with a grad school friend and dating a pretty, upwardly mobile young woman named Mary Schulweiss. When she was offered a great job in California, we decided I'd follow her, and it made sense for us to marry. Within a year after our wedding, she became pregnant. We were so excited we told everyone we knew—and then she miscarried, and our despair was made even worse by having to tell so many people what had happened.

Mary eased her pain by thousands of dollars of retail therapy. I worked overtime and took on extra jobs to dig us out of that debt, and we were out of the hole by the time she became pregnant again.

We didn't tell anyone, not even my father, because we were nervous. And then the worst happened—Mary miscarried again. I was working for a computer company at the time, and part of my job was to make sure our website and intranet were safe from hackers. Studying what they did helped me develop sharp hacking skills myself, and I decided the best way to keep my marriage fiscally sound was to hack into the three main credit bureaus and put a flag on Mary's account, to keep her from racking up more bills.

I got caught and was sentenced to two years in prison. Six months into my term, my father's doctor discovered he had an aggressive form of cancer, which took him away within months. By the time I'd served a year and gotten released on parole, he was dead.

Eric startled me out of my reverie. "I admire him," he said, nodding toward the man in the wheelchair. The oak trees were in new leaf and the sunlight falling through them dappled the street. "Earl Garner. He's the president of the board of directors of the homeowner's association."

"I know the name, but I never connected him with the face," I said. "Why do you admire him? My girlfriend says there are lots of complaints against the property manager and the board. And all you have to do is walk around here to see how long it takes to get the grass cut or the leaves picked up."

"I'm talking about him personally, not the board," Eric said. "He was in law school when he was run over while he was out on his bike. Paralyzed from the waist down. But he fought back, finished law school, started his own practice."

By then Rochester and Gargamel were panting, so we gathered up their leashes and I deliberately led Rochester toward Garner and his son, to get a closer look at this man who I might need to speak with about the name plate letter.

As I got close, though, he swiveled his chair around in a move that reminded me of a Paralympic basketball player, and headed up his driveway. "Come on, sport," he called to his son. "Time for dinner."

His son followed him, and Rochester and I continued down the street. With Lili's comments in my mind, I noticed problems in the community I had failed to in the past. Hedges were trimmed so far down they were barely a collection of sticks. Pavement had eroded in places, with big gaps between yard and street. The lawns had been cut erratically – some sheared down to the ground, while others flourished like miniature jungles.

On our way home, Rochester and I ran into another neighbor, a retired woman named Norah who had recently moved to River Bend from Philadelphia. "I'm thinking we made a bad decision to move here," she said. "Look at this pile of clippings in my yard." She had retained the city's twangy elongated vowel sounds, so it sounded like she had a pal of clippings. "It's been here for a week and nobody's come by to remove it."

"Have you complained to the association?"

"Are you kidding? The secretary makes excuses for the manager, and when he's there on his own he duddnt even answer his phone." She leaned toward me. "And I don't want to go see him because he's already sent me two of those letters about my flowerpots."

She motioned behind her to two huge clay pots, at least three feet in diameter, filled with a cascade of pink daises with red centers. "I don't want to get rid of them, but I'm afraid of the fines. You know if you accrue a high enough fine balance, they can take you to collections and even confiscate your house."

"Can they do really do that?"

"Under Pennsylvania law? They sure can. A friend of mine in a condo in Philly had it happen to her. She was getting confused and forgot to pay her maintenance for a year, and they sued her. Only when her son got an attorney for her did they back off."

I thought back to the woman Lili had mentioned, whose house was in danger of foreclosure. Obviously this threat was a lot greater than just some irritation about a sign. I couldn't imagine what would happen if I lost the house that Lili, Rochester and I called home.

2: A Big Wind

A big wind swept through that evening, shaking some of the dying leaves from the trees and coating the green lawns of River Bend with a crinkly carpet of red, orange, yellow and brown. The same was true all along the River Road, which led up along the Delaware River from Stewart's Crossing to my job at Friar Lake, a conference center owned and operated by Eastern College, where I was the property manager.

An order of Catholic monks had built the complex of buildings, then known as Our Lady of the Waters, over a hundred years before, of local gray stone. When I started at the property, I supervised the renovation of the monks' dormitory into high-tech guest rooms, the conversion of the arched-roof chapel into a reception space, and the expansion of several of the outbuildings into classrooms.

My office was in the former gatehouse, and I pulled up in front of it and let Rochester out. As in River Bend, the lawns were littered with a panorama of fallen leaves. The cobblestone sidewalks and the paved driveway were all covered. Though it looked pretty, it was a trip-and-fall hazard because the leaves masked the steps to the chapel and the delineation between sidewalk and lawn.

I was irritated, because usually the maintenance crew was out early in the morning cleaning up, but I didn't see anyone on the property. I didn't want Friar Lake to end up in the same lousy condition as River Bend.

In our community, it was the responsibility of the landscape company, hired by the board, to cut the lawns and sweep the leaves, to trim the hedges and remove downed tree branches. The board had to hire contractors to repair the sidewalks and repave the streets, especially those areas where tree roots pushed upwards, creating cracks and uneven pavement.

At Friar Lake, I handled the operation of the center, booking conferences and organizing executive education programs. Joey Capodilupo managed the physical plant. He was a skilled jack-of-all-trades handyman who had managed the construction crew that renovated the property. His father was the associate vice president of facilities for Eastern, and after the project was complete Joe Senior had hired his son to keep it going.

Joey had two workmen under him, both Salvadoran immigrants. Where were they? Why weren't they doing their jobs?

Rochester followed me as I headed along a winding path, careful not to slip on leaves slick with morning dew. A square stone building ahead of me housed Joey's office and the maintenance equipment. His truck wasn't parked there, but our laborers, Juan and Rigoberto, were lounging beside an ancient Nissan coupe.

Both wore khaki work pants and Eastern T-shirts. It was a good thing I'd figured out that the name Rigoberto had more letters than Juan and made the connection that the human Rigoberto was bigger than his co-worker, or I'd still be having trouble remembering which was which.

"Sorry, *jefe*, but we no have key to get machines," Rigoberto said. He was the stockier of the two; both had sleek black hair and deeply tanned skin.

After I opened the door for them to get the leaf blowers out of the back, I called Joey's cell phone. Maybe he'd stopped off at the main campus for something and forgotten that Juan and Rigoberto couldn't get into the office.

"Uh, yeah?" Joey said, when he answered.

"Joey, it's Steve. What's up?"

"Oh. Steve. Yeah, right. Um. It's my dad. He had a heart attack last night."

"Oh my God. Is he okay?"

"He's in the hospital now, knocked out and hooked up to a million wires. Doctors said he and my mom did all the right things—he told her as soon as he started feeling bad, she called 911 right away. It looks like he's going to need some bypass surgery, but you know him, he's a tough old bird."

"He is. Listen, I opened the door so the guys can get started blowing the leaves that fell last night. Anything else I can do for you?"

In the background I heard the leaf blowers firing up, and I walked inside Joey's office to get away from the noise.

"Holy crap, I completely lost track of time," Joey said. "My brothers and my mom and I have been here all night. My mom has been trying to shoo my brothers away, it's not like this is a wake or anything. And they've got kids and jobs. She wants me to stay, though."

I looked around Joey's office. His desk was cluttered with filled with piles of paper. A trestle table along one wall had parts of broken equipment in various stages of repair, and the smell of oil and glue hung in the air.

"Call me later when you get a chance to think about anything I can do for you," I said.

He thanked me and hung up, still sounding very distracted. I couldn't blame him, though. I had many regrets over my behavior when I was in California, and one of the biggest was that my incarceration prevented me from spending my dad's last days with him. I couldn't even go to his funeral.

Rigoberto and Juan were blowing leaves off the sidewalk, so I had to detour around them as I walked back to my office in the gatehouse. Rochester kept stopping to sniff the leaves and I had to call him repeatedly. "Don't make me put that leash on you!" I threatened.

He gave me a big doggy grin and romped on ahead of me. I had a lot on my plate at the moment—I had a whole schedule of executive and alumni education programs planned for the fall season, and I needed to stay on top of promotion and registration. I worked with a graphics specialist on the campus who took the information I gave her and prepared a flyer for each event. I had to send in the same information to the web team, who would put it up on a rotating banner on Eastern's home page.

There were endless forms to fill out, for use of the facility (silly, because I was the facility manager, but it had to be done) and for contracts with vendors to provide food for participants. I'd placed an ad for the whole slate of programs in the alumni magazine's September issue, so every day I received several emails or phone calls requesting further information.

Every hour or two I noted the rumble of the leaf blowers as Juan and Rigoberto moved around the property. Shortly before noon a plumber's truck showed up and I had to call Joey once more to see where the problem was, then hang around while the plumber cleared a stopped line in one of the dormitory restrooms.

In between, I needed lunch, and Rochester needed a run around the property. As we sat on one of the picnic benches a chilly breeze swept through, reminding me that winter was coming. I knew there was a long list of things Joey did to get the property prepared for the cold season and hoped he'd be able to manage it. Friar Lake was run so much better than River Bend, and I didn't want to see that change.

It was a busy day, and I realized how much I had come to depend on Joey to keep the physical plant operational. I worried that if he was out with his father for too long, small problems would crop up that I wouldn't notice, which could then cascade into much bigger ones.

I called him late in the afternoon to check on his dad. "They scheduled the bypass surgery for Friday. I'll probably be out the rest of the week with him and my mom."

"Make sure you take care of yourself," I said. "Get some sleep. You won't be much good for your parents if you wear yourself out."

He agreed he would, and I hung up. I had kept the property going a couple of times when Joey went on vacation, but he'd always left me detailed instructions and schedules. I'd have to wing things this week, and I didn't want to bother him too much.

By the time I piled Rochester in the car for our ride home, I was exhausted, but he still needed his dinner and a walk. We took our regular route, a couple of turns along leafy streets to a dead-end with a dog-waste receptacle at the end. Rochester obligingly did his business within a few feet of the bin, shaped like a doghouse with a gaping hole in the center for deposit of bags.

We were on our way home when a man about ten or fifteen years older than I was approached walking a tan and white corgi like the ones Queen Elizabeth favored. Though I didn't recognize the man, Rochester knew the dog immediately, and went down on his front paws in the play position.

The corgi yipped eagerly and tugged the man forward. "Is this Lilibet?" I asked.

"You know her? Yeah, she's my mom's." He motioned behind him. "Sylvia Greenbaum, lives over there on Trieste. She's in the hospital and I'm staying at her house and taking care of the dog."

I could see a bit of resemblance to his mother in the sharp Roman nose, and though he was probably only in his fifties he had the same salt-and-pepper gray hair she did.

Rochester and Lilibet sniffed each other, and the little dog rolled over on her back.

"I hope it's nothing serious," I said.

"She's been losing her mind, bit by bit," the man said. "She fell on a piece of broken sidewalk near the house the other day and broke her hip, so she's going to be in rehab for a while. The apartment where I live doesn't take dogs, so I figured I'd move in here for the time being."

"This is Rochester, and I'm Steve. Please send our love. She's a sweet woman."

"I'm Drew, and obviously you already know Lilibet. You wouldn't say that my mom was sweet if you knew her when she had all her marbles. She was whip smart and had a wicked tongue. Not the most popular gal on the block."

"Did you let the management office know that your mother fell? If the sidewalk is broken it's their responsibility to get it fixed."

"The manager said they can't afford to bring out a repair company for a single problem, but he'd put it on the list and when there were enough repairs to justify the service call, he'd make it."

"That doesn't sound right. This is a safety issue and it ought to take priority."

"I won't repeat the things my mother has said about the management here. Not my circus, not my monkeys. I just need to keep things together until I can get her out of rehab and settled somewhere."

Rochester and Lilibet played for a couple of minutes, and then she decided she was done, jumping up and nipping Rochester on the nose. He looked baffled and backed away. I told Drew I hoped his mom recovered quickly and headed home with Rochester.

As we walked, I wondered what my mother would have been like had she reached her eighties. Like Sylvia Greenbaum, she was very smart, and didn't tolerate fools gladly. She had been a bookkeeper and executive secretary and was quick to leave a job when she felt she wasn't valued enough.

Would she have sweetened up as she got older? Or maybe Sylvia Greenbaum had only gotten nicer as she lost more of her mind. At least my mother hadn't had to suffer that.

As Rochester and I walked up our driveway, I noticed the Levitan sign. It reminded me of my parents and the legacy they had left me. I had photos of the house taken soon after my father bought it, and the sign was there then, so it ought to be grandfathered in.

The term grandfathered had other heavy connections to my father. When I had relayed the news of Mary's first pregnancy to my father, he was so excited. "You did good, Steve," he said. "I always told you I wanted to be a father-in-law before I became a grandfather, and you listened." Too bad he'd never had the chance to be the grandfather he wanted to be.

That sign over the garage was more than just a piece of wood with my name on it. It was one of my last connections to my father, and there was no way I was taking it down.

3: Broken Windows

When I got in, Lili was curled on the couch with her feet under her. "That sounds delicious," she said to her caller. "And apples are in season now."

I liked the sound of "apples" and "delicious" together. While apples were far from my favorite fruit, I was happy to eat them in pies, breads and apple cakes.

I unhooked Rochester's leash and left it hanging from by the doorway on a hook surmounted by a carved golden's head. One of the many golden retriever knickknacks that had invaded my house since Rochester and I met.

"Hold on, he's right here," Lili said to her caller, and held the phone out to me. "It's Tamsen. Or at least it was. Rick wants to talk to you."

Rick Stemper, Tamsen's man-friend, and I had been acquaintances at Pennsbury High, sharing a chemistry course in twelfth grade, and then become friends when I returned to Stewart's Crossing and we bonded over our divorces. He was a detective with the Stewart's Crossing police, and Rochester and I had helped him out a couple of times with his cases.

"I have something I want to run by you. You free to meet up tomorrow at the Chocolate Ear? Say, eight o'clock?"

"Sure," I said. "My partner in crime and I would be happy to consult with you."

"Crime detection, you mean," Rick said with a laugh. He hung up, and I thought about all the times Rochester and I had helped Rick, and his brothers in blue in other jurisdictions, with clues that led to bringing bad guys to justice.

The next morning, instead of having breakfast at home, I drove down into the center of Stewart's Crossing with Rochester. My hometown was charming, the streets lined with Victorian-era homes decorated with lacy white gingerbread, most of them converted to restaurants, doctor's offices or real estate operations. The Chocolate Ear was located in a small stone building on Main Street, with green and white awnings out front, along with a few Parisian-style wrought iron tables and chairs.

I sat back and looked at the traffic moving along Main Street. Mercedes, BMWs and Jaguars, from low-slung sports cars to big SUVs, trailed each other like obedient elephants. The oaks and maples along the sidewalks were turning colors, though the town was doing a better job of picking up fallen leaves than the maintenance crew was doing at River Bend.

A young woman in a sports bra and tight shorts jogged past us, and I was watching her departing figure when Rick slid into the chair across from me. "Enjoying the scenery?" he asked with a smile.

"No harm in looking. Haven't seen you much since we got back from the shore. What's going on?"

Rick, Tamsen and her son Justin had accompanied Lili and me down the shore in August, where we'd had a great week with the dogs.

"Swamped with petty crimes," Rick grumbled. "Broken windows at the florist's greenhouse. Shoplifting at the IGA grocery. Cars at the shopping center broken into."

"Wow, a regular crime wave, here in Stewart's Crossing."

"Don't laugh. It's serious. This is suburban policing, though my boss is taking things to the extreme."

"In what way?" I picked up my café mocha and drained the last few drops. I knew if I ordered a second I'd be wired all day—but maybe I would need that, to do both Joey's job and mine.

Before I could decide, Rick asked, "You ever hear of the broken windows theory of policing?"

"Can't say I have."

"A couple of social scientists came up with this theory back in the 1980s. That if a neighborhood has a lot of petty crime going on like vandalism, litter and broken windows in abandoned buildings, it sends out crime-promoting signals."

I was immediately reminded of the maintenance problems at River Bend. Did that mean we were leaving ourselves open for a crime wave?

"Sounds like what's going on in my neighborhood." I told him about the letter I had received from the association. "It's ridiculous that they're focusing on such tiny things when there are real problems like poor road maintenance and a broken sidewalk that caused an old lady to fall. It's as if they can't see the forest for the trees."

"We're fortunate that all we have are trees in town, then," Rick said. "As you can imagine, Jerry and I are both as busy as hungry dogs with a broken treat jar."

Jerry Vickers was the other detective on the SCPD; I'd met him once or twice.

"Anyway, I wanted to ask you to keep an eye out for anything you see around town. I know you and Rochester are both pretty observant, and if I can get a jump on any problem before they are reported, the chief will be happy."

We talked for a few more minutes, and then Rick's cell buzzed with a call he had to take, so he waved goodbye to me and Rochester and walked back in the direction of the police station.

I looked across Main Street to the Stewart's Crossing shopping center. It had been a thriving place when I was a kid, and I used to bike down there from my parents' house. I'd buy greeting cards at the card store, stare through the window of the laundromat at the clothes swirling around, inhale the scent of pizza from the Italian restaurant.

The tenants had all changed since then, replaced by a cell phone store, a karate dojo, and a tax office. The windows of the space at the end were covered with brown paper and a for rent sign. What looked like fresh graffiti had been spray-painted on the side window facing Main Street.

Another situation for Rick to attack.

It was clear that the problems in my neighborhood were greater than just some small irritations, and that there were larger issues at work. But what could I do about them?

4: Management Issues

When Rochester and I arrived at Friar Lake, I saw Juan and Rigoberto hanging around in front of my office in the gatehouse, the small square stone building that had originally welcomed mendicant friars to Our Lady of the Waters. I realized I was going to have to get there earlier every day that Joey was out, because clearly these guys were not self-motivated.

"What do you want us to do today, *jefe?*" Rigoberto asked.

I had no idea. "Hold on, let me give Joey a call." I pressed the speed dial for Joey's cell while I unlocked the gatehouse. Rochester, Juan and Rigoberto followed me in.

"Did they bag up all the leaves yesterday?" Joey asked as soon as I told him I had Juan and Rigoberto with me.

"Yup."

"Good. Then check the maintenance schedule on the wall in my office. What's today, Thursday?"

"Wednesday."

"Crap. I'm losing track of the days. Anyway, unless there's a program coming in and they have specific work to do for you, on Wednesdays they hose down all the sidewalks, sweep out and dust the chapel, and empty the exterior trash cans and put new bags in. You don't have anything coming up, do you?"

"We've got a catered lunch on Friday for the president's executive council, including the board of directors," I said. "In the chapel."

We had repurposed the original high-ceilinged chapel, with its glorious stained-glass windows, original oak floors and stone walls, to be a reception center. We had movable screens to close off parts of the building—for example, if we had a cocktail party in the front section, we could hide the rear while the caterers set up for a dinner.

"Crap. Walter will be there. He's going to nit-pick everything. If I come over tomorrow afternoon, can you and I do a walk-through?"

"Sure. I'll ask the guys to start with the chapel in case they discover anything that needs more attention."

I had a master key to every lock on the property, so I walked over to the chapel with Juan and Rigoberto, Rochester trailing behind us, and opened it up for them. Rigoberto got a big vacuum cleaner from a storage closet behind the nave, and Juan pulled out a tall ladder and a bunch of cleaning cloths and window spray. I watched Juan position the ladder by the first stained-glass window and scramble up to the top and begin cleaning.

It was important to me, too, that Friar Lake look perfect on Friday. Eastern's president, John William Babson, had taken a chance on me when he hired me to manage the renovation process and then the operation of the center, and I never wanted him to regret that decision.

That fall represented my first full year of programs. I had recruited faculty to teach sessions on everything from contemporary politics to new developments in cancer research. I ran evening events where we discussed classic books led by one of the professors from the English department, one-day workshops on personal financial management, with alumni speakers from banks and investment firms, and a weekend program on building your own bucket list of travel destinations.

Some of the programs I put together bombed, like the debate between two professors about the future of zoos and wildlife preserves. Or maybe our target population was busy that night. It was hard to tell without doing more specific research, which was on my agenda.

I was learning as I went. After each program I surveyed participants about the event itself and asked what else they would like to learn, and I was impressed at the variety of programs they requested.

The seminars on financial management, investments, and retirement planning were perennial favorites, and I had one of those scheduled for the following week. I spent some time that morning following up with my speakers, sending reminders to participants, and doing one last quick email to recruit anyone who was still on the fence.

When I checked my email that afternoon, Joey had forwarded a couple of messages from his boss to me, asking me to handle them. I had to fill out a requisition for cleaning supplies: the maids who kept the dormitory rooms tidy were running out of spray cleaner and rubber gloves. Walter wanted a check on the warranty status of all the mechanical equipment, which required me to go down to Joey's office and look through his files.

As I walked over there, I thought again about my father, who like Joey had been a whiz at carpentry and able to fix anything mechanical. It struck me that years after his death he still popped into my head so often.

Since my father's office was nearly an hour's drive from Stewart's Crossing, I'd never been there, but had always assumed it was as organized as his basement workshop. That was where the resemblance to Joey stopped, though. Joey's office looked like the inside of a crazy clockmaker's head. Bits of wood and wire littered a workbench under the window, along with dissected locks, broken and cracked tiles, and what looked like parts of a hose nozzle.

Three huge piles of papers tottered on his metal desk, with smaller piles beside them, even covering the modern multi-line telephone. It took me most of an hour to dig out the warranty paperwork I spent another couple of hours filing copies of invoices, instruction manuals and business cards from vendors that had been stuck in every crevice. I worried that Joey was overworked. Or was he just poorly organized? Either case presented a problem for the future, something I'd have to address with him once his father was better.

Keeping busy pushed thoughts of the association demand out of my head. It wasn't until Rochester and I had left Friar Lake that evening that my thoughts returned to the issue of the sign over my garage. As we drove down River Road, past a mix of evergreens and the skeletons of deciduous trees, I was able to think clearly and formulate my argument.

When I got back to River Bend, it was four-thirty, and I dropped Rochester at home and walked over to the clubhouse. The evening sky had shaded to a dark gray, and there was a steady stream of sports cars and SUVs along River Bend Drive. A breeze shook a few oak leaves on my head and shoulders as I walked down the sidewalk, which had a long horizontal crack in it. The crack looked like it had been there for a while, based on the oak seedlings popping up through it, which had been tamped down by lots of footsteps.

At least half the parking spaces in the clubhouse lot were taken up by landscaping equipment. Since people were able to rent out the clubhouse for events or come over there to use the swimming pool or take yoga classes, I was surprised that Todd let the landscapers use so much of the parking spaces.

But that wasn't my problem; I wanted to focus on the sign my father had made. My simmering anger popped up again. Why was the association focusing on something as small as my sign, when it seemed like the whole neighborhood was falling apart?

The front door to the clubhouse opened on a hallway that led straight through to the pool area at the rear. The gym was to the right of the front door, where a collection of workout equipment stood along the glass walls, so you could look out to the pool, the parking lot or the nature preserve as you lifted weights or used the treadmill. The open area in the center was used for yoga and tai chi classes, and a pile of mats rested near the door.

The meeting room and the management office were to the left. Todd's secretary Lois was at her desk, and Todd was in his office behind her, on the phone.

Lois was a white-haired woman in her sixties, with red-framed glasses and a matching red beret. It seemed better to start with her rather than directly with Todd, because her sweet nature was matched by the bowl of chocolate candies on the desk in front of her.

I slid into the chair across from her and introduced myself. Though I'd met her a couple of times, there were over seven hundred residents in River Bend, and I didn't expect her to remember all of us.

"I wanted to ask you about this letter I got from the association," I said. "About a sign over my garage that's been there since before I moved in."

"Yes, we've gotten a lot of complaints about those letters," she said. "I'm sorry so many people have gotten upset, but we only work at the direction of the board of directors."

"I understand that it's your company that instituted the fine management software."

"Well, Pennsylvania Property Management purchased the license for the software, but the individual associations decide how it should be deployed." She leaned forward and lowered her voice. "So far, River Bend is the first big community to use it. The revenue that has come in from people paying fines has been substantial, which means the directors are going to keep using it."

She sat back. "But you should really talk to Todd if you have a specific question." She looked down at the phone where a red light had blinked off. "He's off his call, if you want to talk to him."

I stood up and walked behind her desk. Todd had his head down, looking at something on his desk, and I rapped lightly on the door frame.

"Hi," I said, when he looked up. "Steve Levitan, from Sarajevo Way. Could I talk to you for a moment?"

"Sure, come on in."

"I wanted to talk to you about a letter I got," I said, as I sat across from him.

"What kind of letter did you get? Landscaping? Home alterations? Leaving your trash cans out too long?"

"Home alterations, I guess you'd call it." I explained the situation. "That sign has been up since my father first bought the house. I don't understand why someone's complaining about it now."

Todd sat back in his chair. "Lois and I, and PPM in general, work at the direction of the board of directors. They tell us they want to increase association revenue, and we do what we can to accomplish that. There have been some complaints as well that these letters are targeting people who live in their own properties, rather than homes that are rented out. But I will be reviewing all the letters in the next few days to make sure we impose these rules evenly."

"I understand levying people fines for not observing rules, like leaving trash cans out, or not picking up after their dogs. But this kind of nit-picking doesn't sit well. Is there anything I can do to get the sign approved?"

"Do you have any pictures of the house at the time your father bought it?"

"Absolutely."

"Excellent. Pull those out, along with any other relevant information – the time he bought it, the time you inherited, and so on. There's a Design Committee meeting tonight here in the clubhouse, so get here a few minutes before eight o'clock to get yourself on the agenda. Present your documents and if the committee approves the sign, you'll be in compliance, and no fines will be assessed."

As I walked home, I thought that meeting had gone much better than I expected. I understood Todd's position – I'd be in a similar situation when the president's executive council came to lunch at Friar Lake. I hoped there wouldn't be any problems that caused either Joey or me to be called on the carpet.

5: By Design

That night after dinner, I went through the thick set of association by-laws that had been given to my father when he closed on the townhouse. I found the section on design modifications to houses.

"'Homeowner shall have the right to petition the Design Committee for any modifications to the Home's exterior,'" I read out to Lili. "Any such modifications not submitted or approved shall be considered to be in violation of these By-Laws."

"Sounds pretty clear to me," Lili said.

"But wait. 'Association shall have a period of one year to contest any violations and be authorized to collect fines as spelled out in these By-Laws. If a period of one year passes without contest, the modifications shall be considered approved.' I've certainly been here longer than that."

"Well, there you go," Lili said. "It pays to read these things through. I've had to nearly memorize the faculty collective bargaining agreement in order to mediate problems that come up with my staff."

At a few minutes before eight, I walked over to the clubhouse, picked up a copy of the agenda and signed my name to the list of those who wanted to address the committee. There were already ten other homeowners in front of me, and I joined the crowd and sat down.

Through the glass window, I could see Todd Chatzky at his

computer with a headset on, as if he was either listening to music or participating in a conference call. I wondered why he was in there instead of out in the main clubhouse at the meeting.

The four members of the committee sat behind a long table at the front of the room. I looked at the agenda, which listed the members by name. By process of elimination the sole woman was Kimberly Eccles. I recognized Earl Garner, in his wheelchair, which left two other men: Oscar Panaccio and Vern DeSimone.

Panaccio's name sounded familiar, and while I waited for things to begin I opened Eastern's website on my phone and discovered that Panaccio was a professor of sociology. A quick search revealed that he lived in a house on Bucharest Place, at the other end of River Bend from mine. That meant the other man was DeSimone.

One by one, my neighbors stood up and made their cases. One man who owned a single-family house had painted his front door black. "My house is for sale, and I'm trying to maximize my value." He put on a pair of narrow glasses and read from a sheet of paper. "I'm quoting from *Money* magazine, June 20th. Zillow found that on average, houses with black or charcoal gray front doors sold for as much as $6,271 more than expected."

"That's not the point," Garner said. "The association design guidelines are very clear. Every front door must be painted white."

"I'll paint it back as soon as it sells," the man argued.

"Request denied." Garner looked down at the list and called the next name.

"You all are a bunch of assholes," the door man said, and he stalked out.

The rejections came quickly, with little discussion. A woman with a profusion of orchids hanging from the oak tree in front of her house was chastised and allowed to retain one basket in her front yard. Kimberly Eccles suggested she move the rest to her back yard, where she could still enjoy them.

A man with a damaged garage door was given sixty days to have it replaced. A woman who had put ornamental stones around the oak in her front yard had to remove them.

Todd Chatzky came out of his office as the woman was leaving, and pulled up a chair beside the committee table. His eyes sagged as if he was very tired, and sweat stained the underarms of his gray and white houndstooth check shirt.

"Sorry to be late, but Pennsylvania Properties is working on some big changes to the way we operate, and I had to sit in on a long conference call."

"That's never good news, when you people start to stick your foot into things," Panaccio said. I was glad I'd never had to take a class with him or serve on a committee at Eastern with him.

Next up was Drew Greenbaum. "I'm here on behalf of my mom, who's in the hospital right now," he said. "I've been going through her bills and paperwork and I found this series of complaints from the association." He held up a sheaf of papers. "My mother is eighty-give years old, and you guys are harassing her over a bird feeder in her front yard."

"What's your point?" Earl Garner asked. "Take down the bird feeder and you solve the problem."

"You'll drop the lawsuit?" Greenbaum asked.

"Hold on. There's a lawsuit?" Oscar Panaccio asked.

Greenbaum nodded. "It's more than just the bird feeder," he admitted. "She's been sick, like I said, so she hasn't been able to keep up the property to your standards. The house needs to be painted, one of the second-floor windows is broken, and there are some loose roof tiles. The fines mounted up and last month the association put a lien on the property for the amount of the fines."

He fidgeted in his seat. "I'm hoping you can cut us some slack because my mom has been diagnosed with Alzheimer's, so she probably didn't understand the notices she got. And you guys have left a piece of sidewalk near her house broken, and she fell there."

"Don't threaten us with a liability lawsuit," Garner said. "I'm an attorney and there's no way you can win unless you have video of her falling. You have that?"

Drew frowned. "Nope. But come on, I need to sell the house so I can put her in a memory-care assisted living facility, but I can't sell it with the lien against it."

"Then pay off the lien," Garner said.

"With what money?" Greenbaum was exasperated. "My mother lives on Social Security and I'm unemployed."

"This isn't a matter for the design committee," Garner said. "Talk to me after the meeting and I'll see what I can do for you."

"I'm starting to feel like whole purpose of this committee is to screw over our residents," Kimberly Eccles said. "This is a terrible situation. Can't we do something?"

I smiled. Maybe there was hope for Drew, if the committee would act in a reasonable manner.

"You don't want to set a bad precedent," Panaccio said. "You make one exception, then everyone else wants one, and the whole community goes to pot."

"It already has," DeSimone said. "I know where that lady fell. I reported it to Todd six months ago. We're nit-picking people with flowers when this whole place is falling down around our heads."

There went my idea of the committee acting reasonably.

"We're getting off track here," Todd said, in a sharp voice. "If you have safety concerns about the property, those need to be brought before the safety and security committee. When this issue first came up, that's where I directed the question. I can't spend the money to hire a contractor for a problem like that without authorization from the board, and the way the by-laws are written the safety committee has to make the recommendation to the board."

"And did they? I don't remember that," Eccles said.

"I'll have Lois check the minutes tomorrow," Todd said.

There was some general grumbling from the audience, but Todd glared until everyone was quiet again. Then he turned to the committee. "Please return to the issue at hand. The rules are clear. There isn't anything the board can do once a lien has been placed against a homeowner. Mr. Greenbaum will have to take out a mortgage against his mother's property to pay off the lien or find a private buyer who will agree to pay off the lien."

"How can you people be so heartless?" Greenbaum demanded. "My mother has lived here since River Bend was built."

Earl Garner slammed his gavel against the table. "You heard the property manager. There's nothing the association can do. We need to move on."

Greenbaum stormed out of the building, hurling curses at Todd and the committee. I was glad that I wasn't up next, because the committee and the crowd were still agitated, and the next homeowner was turned down almost immediately.

When my name was called, I handed each committee member the pages I had printed for them—my father's deed, and the transfer to my name and several pictures of the house from different angles, that were date stamped soon after his purchase, and showed the sign in question.

"Because this sign was clearly visible over five years ago, it's has been grandfathered in," I said. "I'd like a letter from the association confirming that."

"There's no such thing as grandfathering," Panaccio said.

"There is, according to section five, paragraph three of the by-laws." I handed each of them a copy of the relevant section, and Garner, the attorney, read through it quickly.

"It appears there is," he said, when he looked up. "I'll have to make a note to the by-laws committee to review this so that we don't have to make exceptions like this in the future. Request granted."

Panaccio started to complain but Garner looked at him. "You may be a biologist, but you can read, can't you, Oscar? The paragraph is pretty clear."

Garner and Panaccio began arguing. I looked over at Todd Chatzky, and he nodded at me, so I stood up and walked out.

One small victory for the little guy, I thought, as I walked home. If only all my problems could be solved so easily.

6: Dark Discovery

I should have been happy that night. I'd won my small victory over the design committee. I was taking care of Joey's responsibilities at Friar Lake. And I'd begun the process of bringing in more revenue.

But I found it hard to sleep. I worried about the future—how long could I hold on to my job, especially if I couldn't do what President Babson wanted? If I had a heart attack like Joe Capodilupo, how could Lili manage to look after me and Rochester? I remembered a cartoon I'd seen online, an old man with a cane, who said, "Oh, crap, I forgot to have children to take care of me in my old age."

When the clock's digits finally clicked over to five am, I gave up and slipped out of bed. I dressed quietly so I wouldn't disturb Lili, and padded downstairs, Rochester right behind me. I grabbed a flashlight and a plastic grocery bag and hooked up his leash.

The crescent moon looked like a courtesan resting on her back, the stars her attendants. A couple of houses had front lights on, and I saw the occasional light in a house, usually in an upper window behind glass blocks, which indicated a bathroom. For the most part, though, River Bend looked like the early scenes before an attack in one of those disaster movies, eerily quiet and empty.

Maybe because the side streets were so dark, Rochester was determined to walk along River Bend Drive, where period streetlamps reminded me of those from the Narnia books and movies. I half-expected Mr. Tumnus the faun to step out from behind one.

Much of the area close to the Delaware north of Stewart's Crossing was swampy with a high water table. When River Bend was built, the developer had dredged a series of lakes, using the fill to build up the land for homes and townhouses. The centerpiece of the neighborhood was a pair of lakes with a tree-lined walkway between them. I took Rochester there only occasionally, because it was a long hike from Sarajevo Street.

That night, though, we both needed a good long walk. During the day we often saw birds there and the occasional small mammal, but there were no signs of life as we approached, not even the warning call of a bird or a duck.

We approached the pathway between the lakes, where a series of benches lined the path, facing each other at intervals. At night they were dark, boxy shapes that held a hint of menace, and I tried to hurry Rochester along. Something made him stop at one of the benches. It looked like a sprinkler had gone off in the middle of the night, leaving the pavement wet, and he wanted to sniff it.

Then a slight wind picked up, moving the night smells along, and I realized from the coppery tang in the air that it wasn't water on the pavement. It was blood.

I tugged Rochester's leash and pulled him back. With my hand low and tight around the flat cord, I took my phone out of my pocket and stepped closer. I initiated the flashlight app and used the light to follow the bloody trail that led beneath the bench. A two-foot wide space was between the back of the bench and the hedge that separated it from the lake behind.

A man's body rested on the dirt behind the bench. "Oh my God," I said. "Hello? Are you okay?"

There was no response except a low woof from Rochester. The bloody trail led back to the man's stomach, which looked like it had been ripped open with a knife. I watched him for a moment, looking for a rise and fall of his chest, no matter how slight, but I couldn't see anything.

If he was dead, then this was a crime scene, and I didn't want to get close to him and contaminate it. If he was alive, there was nothing I could do to help him, with only rudimentary first aid skills. So I called 911.

"Please state the nature of your emergency," a nearly robotic female voice said.

"I'm on River Bend Drive in Stewart's Crossing and I found a man who has been stabbed," I said, struggling to keep a quaver from my voice.

"Is he still breathing?"

"I don't think so. There's a lot of blood around his stomach, but it's not still coming out of the body."

"Step away from the body," the woman said. "Give me your exact address."

"There isn't an exact address," I said. "I'm somewhere between Trieste and Zagreb."

"Trieste, Italy?"

"No. Trieste Drive and Zagreb Way. In Stewart's Crossing. Use Google Maps if you can't find it."

"I am dispatching an ambulance and a police officer," she said. "Please remain on the line."

"I have to call the community security," I said. "I'll wait here for the police."

I ended the call and pressed the button for the gatehouse at the Ferry Street entrance. "My name is Steve Levitan and I'm standing with my dog on the sidewalk between the two big lakes, off River Bend Drive. Can you please send the rover over here? There's a dead man behind one of the benches."

"Stay where you are," the guard said. "I'll have the rover come right over."

One of the advantages of living in a gated community is that in addition to the guard at the gate, we have another who rides around the property, keeping an eye out for trouble. But by leaving the body hidden between the bench and the hedge, the killer had managed to keep the rover from noticing anything.

I looked back at the body, trying to see if I recognized him. His face was turned away from me, but I could establish that he was white, wearing dark slacks and a light-colored shirt in a pattern I couldn't make out in the dim light. From the curled position of the body I couldn't tell how tall he was, but he appeared to have an average build—not too slim, but not heavyset either.

Rochester kept straining toward the blood, and I had to take a couple of steps back. I sat on the opposite bench, petting his fur and letting his presence calm me, until I saw the green and yellow light bar on top of the rover's SUV. I stood up and waved my phone toward the car, letting the flashlight beam bounce from tree to hedge.

The guard driving the rover parked at one end of the sidewalk and came up toward me, playing his flashlight on the pavement in front of him. He was a young African-American guy, barely older than the students at Eastern, and he looked nervous. "There's a dead man here?" he asked.

I pointed my flashlight toward the bench. "Behind there. I already called 911."

He stepped close, and I was about to warn him not to contaminate the scene when he stopped and shone his flashlight on the body. Then he stepped back and turned to me. "You were out walking your dog this early in the morning?"

"Couldn't sleep. He sniffed the blood there and tugged me over." I didn't want to confuse the situation by noting that this was not the first dead body Rochester had found.

We stood together in an uneasy silence until his radio

crackled. "Rover one, this is Ferry Gate. Ambulance on its way to your location."

We both turned toward Ferry Street and watched as the lights of the ambulance approached. Before it came to a stop there was another call from the gate, that a police car was on its way as well.

I knew what was going to happen because I'd seen it before. Stewart's Crossing didn't have its own crime scene investigation unit; they would have to rely on one from the state police. A detective from the Stewart's Crossing PD, either Rick or Jerry Vickers, would be summoned to the scene, depending on which was on call.

I decided to take control of that process and called Rick's cell phone. He was usually at his desk by seven-thirty, and often rose early to go for a run, so I didn't feel too bad about waking him—it was nearly five-thirty by then.

"What?" he said sleepily.

"Dead body. River Bend. Can you take it?"

"Oh, Steve. You're killing me, you know that?"

"I know. I don't like this any more than you do."

"On my way. I'll call dispatch and take it."

The ambulance parked behind the rover's SUV, and a pair of EMTs, a tall man and a shorter woman, approached us. Both were barely older than the security guard.

"He's behind the bench," I said, pointing, and the guard and I stepped out of their way.

The female EMT squeezed behind the bench, careful not to step in blood, and tried to take the man's vital signs. Then she spoke into the radio on her shoulder. "At the scene on River Bend Drive. No sign of life."

She stood as the police car pulled up. The officer who approached us was about the same age as the guard and the EMTs, and I felt old. "I'll call for a detective and the crime scene unit," he said. "No one touch anything, okay?"

I stood around awkwardly with the police officer, the security guard and the two EMTs. The female made friends with Rochester, squatting down to pet him, and he was happy with the attention.

The cop turned to me and the security guard. "Either of you recognize the man?"

"Can't see his face, the way he's turned," I said. He had to be a River Bend resident, didn't he? Who else would be on foot in the community in the middle of the night? There was no guest parking area nearby. The security patrol had been aggressive in ticketing cars parked there overnight, which was against yet another of the rules, so if he'd come in and parked, they ought to find the car eventually.

Two more police cars arrived, and the officers moved us down the sidewalk and set up a cordon around the area. Close to six o'clock, Rick arrived in his truck. He greeted the officers and the EMT, and then walked down to where I had been told to wait, by the farthest bench from the body.

"The CSI team is coming from the State Police barracks in Trevose," he said. "Should be here within a half hour. Tell me exactly what happened."

"I couldn't sleep, so I got up at five to take Rochester for his walk," I said. "It was dark and creepy, and Rochester wanted to stay where there are streetlights, so we walked up along River Bend Drive."

I took a deep breath. "I didn't see any people or vehicles out as we came over here. Rochester tugged me along the path between then lakes, and then stopped at a pile of something liquid."

Despite the number of times this sort of thing had happened to me, it was still difficult to report. "At first I thought it was a malfunctioning sprinkler, but then the wind shifted and I smelled the blood. He kept tugging me toward the bench, and when I shone a light I saw the body and I reined him in before he could get close enough to disturb anything."

I was relieved to come to the end of the story. "I called 911 and then the front gate. Then you. That's all I can say."

"You don't know who it is?"

I shook my head. "Couldn't see the face." I visualized the body in my mind again, and something nagged at me about the pattern on the man's gray shirt. Where had I seen that before? I concentrated, and Rochester nuzzled me, and then I remembered the houndstooth pattern I'd seen earlier that day.

"I think I know who it is," I said.

7: Houndstooth

"Well, don't keep a secret," Rick said. "Who is it?"

"I can't be a hundred percent sure without seeing his face, but I think it's Todd Chatzky. He's the association manager, and he came to a meeting last night of the design committee."

I quickly ran through the letter I'd gotten and my victory. "Todd showed up toward the end of the meeting, and he was wearing a shirt with a houndstooth pattern. I remember looking at it and thinking that was a good sign, you know, the way those checks look like the edge of a dog's tooth?" I knew I was rambling and took a deep breath.

"Stay here for a minute," Rick said.

As he walked back toward the body, he fiddled with his cell phone, and then he used the flashlight as he knelt beside it, staying clear of the blood trail. Then he walked back to me. "Yeah, I checked the pattern online and it's houndstooth. Seen that kind of pattern, but never made the connection before."

He sat down beside me, and Rochester nuzzled his leg. "Tell me what you know about this manager guy."

I ran through some of the problems going on in River Bend while we waited for the CSI team to arrive. "Lili turned me on to this online site called Hi, Neighbor. I haven't looked at it too closely, but I've seen a lot of complaints posted by people who live here." I mentioned some of the ongoing issues, like the inattention to landscaping, the broken sidewalk, and the fine management program.

"Sounds like a lot of people were unhappy with Mr. Chatzky," Rick said when I finished.

"Unhappy, yeah. Like wanting to get him fired. Not killed." I shivered. "There were a couple of people who said things at the meeting last night, but nothing serious."

"Tell me," Rick coaxed.

I explained the problem of the man with the black door, and how he had told the committee to fuck off and die. "I know, it's not a real threat. I'm just repeating it."

Then I told him about the Yiddish curse Drew Greenbaum had used.

"A sugar rope? Really? Do they even make something like that?"

I shrugged. "Maybe back in the old country. Most of the Yiddish phrases my parents used didn't make any sense. I remember my mother used to have this phrase when she thought something was useless. When I asked her what it meant, she had to go into a long business about how doctors used to use leeches on sick people, and this phrase was that it was as useful as using leeches on the dead."

"You Jews certainly have colorful language," Rick said. "The worst thing my father ever said to me when I was misbehaving was 'I hope you grow up to have children like you.'"

"Yeah, my parents said that one, too. I used to counter my father with 'I hope I don't have a child like you!'"

I shrugged. "Guess neither of us are going to have that problem."

"I don't know. If I marry Tamsen, I'll get to help raise Justin as he goes through adolescence."

"Feel free to complain anytime, then."

The sun was rising, and River Bend was waking up, the streets beginning to fill up with early morning dog walkers, parents taking their kids to school, and people leaving for work. Lots of cars slowed down as they passed the cluster of official vehicles, but the security guard kept them moving.

The CSI team arrived and began their work, Rick stood up to walk over to them. I texted Lili that Rochester and I were sitting out by the lake looking at the sunrise—which was true, though not the whole story. I'd tell her the rest when I saw her.

Rick asked me to stay until the CSI team was able to turn the body so that the man's head was visible. "Just confirm for me what you told me," he said. "That it's Mr. Chatzky."

When he was ready, I walked over with him, keeping Rochester's leash tight. "Yeah, that's Todd," I said.

"All right. You go home. Have some hot tea, get a good breakfast in you. You'll feel better after that. I'll get in touch with you later to learn more about this Hi Neighbor site."

I agreed and walked Rochester back home. Fortunately, he'd done his business before we discovered Todd's body, so we were able to move quickly. Even so, Lili was up in the kitchen waiting for us. "You were gone a long time," she said.

I sat at the kitchen table. The sense of what I'd seen caught up with me, and I didn't think I could move for a while. "Can you feed Rochester and make me some tea?" I asked. "And then I'll tell you."

She poured chow in a bowl for Rochester and sprinkled it with a packet of probiotic dust, then put it down for him. She put the teakettle on the stove and then came to sit across from me. "What's wrong?"

Slowly, I told her everything that had happened that morning. "Oh, Steve," she said, and she took my hand. "How terrible."

I was glad that she didn't complain that Rochester kept finding bodies. I wasn't ready for any kind of light-hearted comment.

"I know there was nothing I could do for him by the time we found him, but I still feel pretty awful."

"You should call in sick today," she said. "Stay home, take a nap, play with Rochester."

"I can't. Joey's out with his father and somebody's got to manage Friar Lake."

I looked at the clock. It was hard to realize that only two hours had passed since Rochester and I began walking down the sidewalk between the lakes. "I'd better get a move on. Rigoberto and Juan get there at seven-thirty and they'll stand around with no one to tell them what to do."

"Give me your phone. Joey can go up there for the morning and see his dad in the afternoon."

I handed her the phone, and she spoke to Joey while she poured my tea. "That's taken care of. He'll be there until noon. Now, I'm going to make you breakfast. We still have some lox left over from Sunday's bagels, so I'll make you lox and eggs, and then you'll take a nap, all right?"

"Yes, love," I said. By the time I was finished with breakfast, I was yawning, so I went upstairs and crawled under the covers, with Rochester on the bed beside me. I stroked his golden head, and before I knew it I was asleep.

By the time I woke, nearly two hours later, Lili had long since left for work. I'd gotten a text from Joey that he was at Friar Lake and everything was fine. I got up and took a shower, and as I was getting dressed Rick called me. "You already at work?" he asked.

"Nope, I took a nap for a while. Just getting ready to go now."

"You think I could come over and talk for a few minutes?"

"Sure. I don't have to be up at Friar Lake until noon."

He arrived a few minutes later, and while he headed for the kitchen table I got my laptop and joined him there. "I've been in the management office," he said. "You know Mr. Chatzky's secretary, Lois?"

I nodded.

"She's pretty broken up. She gave me a whole file of complaints people had made about her boss – both paper and digital. Then she had to shut the office down and go home to rest. There are a lot of bad feelings going on around here."

"To put it mildly." While I spoke, I turned on my laptop and brought up the Hi Neighbor site. "Let me show you what's been happening online."

Once I was able to log in to Hi Neighbor, I turned the screen so Rick could see it. "Wow. That's a lot of messages," he said, as I scrolled through them.

"I can go through them for you this evening," I said. "Pull out the specific issues and which neighbor is complaining about them."

"That would be great." He sat forward in his chair and pulled out the pocket notebook he carried, along with a pen. I noticed that he'd upgraded since meeting Tamsen, who sold advertising specialties. The ones he used now were fancier, with leather covers embossed with corporate logos – product samples, he had told me once. His pen was a gold Cross with a different logo on the body. "Tell me again about last night. You went to a meeting?"

Rick took notes as I ran through my attendance at the design committee meeting, and the way Todd had showed up near the end. "About what time do you think that was?"

"The meeting was called for eight," I said. "We started a few minutes late, and then ran through a bunch of complains. It had to be at least eight-thirty before Todd showed up. He talked for a couple of minutes, and then—"

"Hold on," Rick interrupted. "What did he talk about?"

"Apologized for being late. Said he was on a conference call about changes that came down from Pennsylvania Properties, the company our association hires to manage River Bend. Todd and Lois work for them."

He made more notes. "Did he say what kind of changes those

would be?"

I struggled to remember. "Nothing specific. My case came up after that, and I got the approval I wanted, so I left. When I got home Lili was watching a program on TV in the living room. It was about nine o'clock by then."

Rick closed his notebook. "I spoke with Mr. Garner this morning. He says that the meeting finished around nine-thirty, but he and Mr. Oscar Panaccio stayed around for a few minutes to talk with Mr. Chatzky about the procedural changes he had learned about on his call."

"Did he say what they are?"

"Chatzky wouldn't say – or at least that's what Garner told me. Garner said that Panaccio and Chatzky argued, and Panaccio left angrily."

"Throwing Oscar Panaccio under the bus."

"Well, nobody's a clear suspect yet. There are, what, over seven hundred homes in this community? That's a lot of people with opportunity."

"River Bend keeps a record of every visitor," I said. "You can check with the guard at the gatehouse and get a list of who else was here last night."

"This isn't my first time at the rodeo," Rick said drily. "I've already put that request in. But they only request ID from the driver, not the passengers, so there could be even more people in the area than we know about."

"I'll do what I can with the information from Hi Neighbor to see who has a motive," I said. "Maybe that will help you narrow things down."

"I could use some narrowing," Rick said. "Right now the medical examiner puts the time of death at sometime between nine PM and three AM, though he hopes to get a better estimate after the autopsy. I've got a lot of time to account for and a lot more people to interview."

Rick left, his next stop to see Todd's widow, an orthodontist with an office on Main Street in Stewart's Crossing. I didn't envy him that visit.

8: Speculation

By the time I got to Friar Lake it was close to noon. I parked in front of my office and walked down to Joey's building with Rochester. I found him at his desk, with a file folder open in front of him. "Thanks for doing all my filing," he said, holding up the folder. "It was getting away from me."

"You're welcome. And thank you coming in." I slid into the chair across from him and Rochester sprawled at my feet. "I had a rough morning."

"So Lili said. You found a dead body?"

"Well, Rochester led me there," I said. My golden boy looked up at the sound of his name, and I reached down to stroke the soft down at the top of his head. "The guy was the property manager for our homeowner's association."

"That's awful. The police don't think you killed him, do they?"

I shook my head. "He'd been dead for a couple of hours by then." I shivered, despite the warm air inside Joey's office. "So, how's your dad?"

"He's getting ready for surgery tomorrow. His heart rate and his blood pressure are stable, though he's still hooked up to a bunch of monitors."

"How do you want me to manage Juan and Rigoberto while you're gone?"

"Usually I just tell Juan and Rigoberto what to do every day, but I put together a list for you to follow with them. And I want to come back tomorrow afternoon so you and I can do a final run-through of the property before the executive committee meeting on Friday."

"That would be great."

We walked outside, where he beeped open his truck, and Rochester sat by my side. "Send my regards to your dad," I said, as he hopped inside.

"Will do," he called.

I went into my office, where I found the detailed list Joey had assembled for me. I felt I could follow all that. I caught up on my own emails and paperwork, and before I knew it, five o'clock had rolled around and I drove back home with Rochester.

When he and I walked around River Bend that evening, everyone I met wanted to talk about Todd's murder. That is, all the humans; the dogs were happy to sniff each other, bark and play. The first pair we spotted was Mindy Ebersol and Angel, a fluffy white Coton de Tulear who would only let Rochester sniff for a minute or two before barking to assert his dominance.

"Did you hear about Todd?" Mindy asked. She was an accountant in her twenties who favored crop tops and short shorts to show off her gym-toned body. She wore her blonde hair in a ponytail on the top of her head that reminded me of Pebbles Flintstone.

"I did," I said. "It's terrible."

"I heard he was killed right here in River Bend," she said, with a shiver. "Do you think it was a mob hit?"

My jaw dropped open. "Like the Mafia or something? What makes you say that?"

"My friend Susan lives in South Philly and she's always talking about the Mafia, and how they infiltrate everywhere, from prostitution to soda deliveries. Maybe they're trying to move in on association management."

"I doubt it. But I'm sure the police will check everyone who came in or out last night."

"It's creepy," Mindy said, as Angel began to bark and Rochester backed away. "I moved out here to the suburbs to get away from crime and it followed me here."

I was only a bit astonished at the way she had personalized the crime, even though it had nothing to do with her. Many Eastern students were the same way, assuming that the College and the world were out to get them when they disagreed with a new rule.

"Don't take it too hard. I'm sure the police will find out who did it."

A couple of minutes later we rounded a corner and ran into Eric Hoenigman and Gargamel. We both unclipped our dogs' leashes and Rochester and the big English setter romped through one of the open lots between pods of townhouses. The grass was up to their ankles, and Eric said, "I hope the new property manager leans on the landscapers better."

Man, Todd was barely cold at the Medical Examiner's office and Eric was already talking about his replacement. "I hope so, too."

"I wouldn't be surprised if it was the landscape contractor who killed him," Eric said. "I heard that Todd was always arguing with him."

"Really? How'd you hear that?"

He shrugged. "Just one of those things you hear, walking around. Makes me glad I'm an engineer and I never have to talk to clients or suppliers. Just sit at my computer with my headphones on and put pieces together."

He called Gargamel over and Rochester followed. We hooked up their leashes again and Rochester and I went in the opposite direction, toward home. We passed Norah, the neighbor who'd been worried about having to remove her big clay pots, and she expressed relief that Todd was dead. "He was a jerk and I for one won't miss him," she said. "They need to get a woman in that job. Women are more collaborative and willing to work together to find solutions to problems."

Poor Todd, I thought, after we left Norah. He had started out so well at River Bend, and I thought at heart he was a good guy in a tough situation. But none of the neighbors at River Bend seemed like they'd miss him, and no one seemed to care that he was a human being whose life had been extinguished much too early.

As Rochester and I returned up Sarajevo Court, I spotted Bob Freehl, a neighbor whose house sported a yellow circle on its garage. It was supposed to be an indication to the landscapers to skip his house, because he did all the planting, trimming and grass-cutting himself, but he'd complained in the past that the dumb crew ignored it.

Every tree and flowering plant in his yard was perfectly separated from its neighbor, like a little kid who refused to let different foods touch each other. I noticed for the first time that there was theme to his yard as well, the flowers graduating in size from the tiny pansies we called Johnny-jump-ups to daises and black-eyed Susans.

"You heard about the property manager, I guess," Bob said. He'd been planting a gold chrysanthemum in his front yard, and he stood up and wiped his hands on his faded jeans.

Because Bob was a retired cop, I felt comfortable telling him that I had found the body early that morning.

"I heard it was one of the neighbors, but I didn't get your name," he said. I figured Bob must still have his sources at the department. "This keeps up, we're going to need our own CSI team for Stewart's Crossing."

"One murder isn't a streak," I said.

"It's only one murder, but the crime in this little town is skyrocketing," Bob said. "You gotta pay attention, Steve. Burglaries, vandalism, all those little things start to add up."

"Broken windows," I said.

He looked at me curiously. "You know about that theory?"

"The way I understand, if the police pay attention to the little problems then criminals will be less inclined to act."

"That's the idea, at least," Bob said, nodding. "Though with somebody getting murdered practically in our back yard it may be too late for that."

I didn't think Stewart's Crossing was turning into a hot spot for crime, though I had to agree with Bob that there had been a lot of small incidents in the recent past. When we got home and I sat down to dinner with Lili, I asked what she thought about that

"I've been in a lot of desperate places around the world," she said. "And in every one of them, the police had lost control of the big crimes, as well as the small ones. Though in places like Afghanistan and Nicaragua there were much larger forces at work. I doubt there's a lot of political unrest in Stewart's Crossing that could lead to a crime spree."

"And yet, there are so many problems people are complaining about, on the street and on that Hi Neighbor site. Don't you think that's the first step in bigger crimes?"

"Like Todd Chatzky's murder? I don't follow the logic there."

"I guess what I mean is that when little things go wrong, they start to accumulate, and people get more and more angry. Then bad things happen. Drew Greenbaum's mother fell over a broken piece of sidewalk and now she's going to end up in a nursing home. Something small leads to something larger. I'm not necessarily saying that bad landscaping can lead to murder, but it's hard not to make some connection."

Lili gave me her password and sign-in for Hi Neighbor, and after she went upstairs to read, I settled down with my laptop at the dining room table to take a closer look at the complaints on the website, as I had promised Rick.

Over three hundred messages had come in since Lili signed up for the site a few months before. There was no export feature for the material there, and people often changed the subject line of their messages even when they were following up on a comment about a specific problem, so it looked like it was going to be a big project to review all the material.

I decided I ought to go back to the earliest message and see what I could pick up, but before I did I took a glance at the most recent issues. Drew Greenbaum asked if any other homeowners had dealt with liens against their properties, but no on had responded.

I sat back from the computer. The poor guy was stuck in a very bad position. At least Earl Garner had volunteered to help him, until Todd shut him down. I wondered if Greenbaum had followed up with Todd, maybe later that evening after the meeting was over. He'd certainly been angry. Could that anger have led to violence?

What were any of us capable of, after all? Look at me. I'd been pushed to my limit after Mary's second miscarriage, and though I knew what I was doing was illegal, I'd let my emotions tug me into hacking those databases. If I'd been pushed in a different direction, could I have killed someone, in the heat of the moment?

Though I felt sorry for Drew Greenbaum, I put him first on the list of suspects I was collecting for Rick. I wasn't sure if he had any of the three criteria: means, motive and opportunity. But he was angry enough that if he'd gone home, stewed over his problems for a while, and then gone in search of Todd, with a knife to emphasize his threat—well, who knew what could have happened.

From what Rick had told me in the past, a knife was a very personal way to kill someone. You had to get up close and physically stick the blade in, past layers of skin and flesh. It wasn't like a gun, which you could fire from a few feet away without the visceral connection.

That kind of speculation always made me feel nauseous, so

I pushed it away and went back to what I did best, collecting and organizing information. I created a spreadsheet and worked on the posts from Hi Neighbor for a couple of hours, organizing neighbors by complaints. It was too early to see any patterns, but I knew that it would take patience and work to draw real information out of the data.

I couldn't figure out how to use any of the software tools I had at my disposal to speed up the process. I could have initiated a program to look for key words, for example, but I didn't know what the key words were until I read more of the data. Though there were certain terms that popped up, like paint and grass, too often they were used in other contexts.

From the details they provided, I recognized several neighbors I knew by sight but had never spoken to. An older man on Zagreb Lane who had a long line of azaleas that wrapped around the front and sides of his house, who was always outside watering, trimming or weeding them. A competitive cyclist who wore a skin-tight top advertising Emirates Airlines. A skinny woman in her sixties who ran every morning, and whose business cards advertised her as "Your Running Realtor."

All of them were either complaining, or the subject of complaints. Several people said the cyclist had nearly run them down, while the runner catalogued every landscaping problem she noticed on her trips through the community.

I also recognized a woman I thought of as "the power walker." I had seen her many times, pumping her arms as she speed-walked down the street. I had no gripe against her because she was always aware of her surroundings, unlike other walkers whose attention was glued to their phones. She crossed the street whenever she saw a dog or a group of kids playing.

She came up in a post by her husband, Zane Spahr. He said that his wife, Rosemary, had complained numerous times about potholes in the street. A few days before, she had been walking and stumbled over one of those places where the street was damaged. She had fallen and fractured her tibia. They had filed a complaint with Pennsylvania Properties, but Todd claimed that he couldn't do anything without the approval of the board.

Zane Spahr didn't believe that. His lawyer had warned him that suing the association could have negative effects on his own property values and those of his neighbors, if the association had to pay a settlement. Insurance rates for the association would go up if negligence was proved.

Even so, he threatened to follow through with a lawsuit if the association's insurance carrier wouldn't pay his wife's bills, and his anger radiated from the screen. The last line of his latest post was "The next time I see Todd Chatzky I'm going to make sure he hurts as much as Rosemary."

Not exactly a death threat, but once again, a time when anger could have taken over common sense and led to Todd's death.

Rochester nudged me to remind me it was time for his bedtime walk. Mindful of what had happened to Rosemary Spahr, I took a flashlight with me, shining it ahead of us as we walked to make sure no pothole or pile of debris came into our path.

9: Suspect List

Thursday morning dawned rainy and windy, and I had to hurry Rochester through his morning walk, turning around as soon as he finished his business. Then we shared a rowdy few minutes in the kitchen as I tried to dry him and he preferred to shake all over me. Good times.

He was still damp by the time we had finished breakfast, so I hung a big towel from the headrest on the passenger seat of the BMW. Instead of settling in easily, he pawed it and rolled around until he had created a cushion beneath his butt. "Happy now?" I asked before I put the car in gear.

He looked up at me mournfully, and I couldn't help laughing.

It hadn't rained up at Friar Lake, and that morning, Rochester and I walked all around Friar Lake looking for potential problem areas. I tried to look at everything through Joey's eyes instead of my own, focusing on the physical plant.

Leaves were strewn on the curving road that led up to the hilltop property. Technically, those were the responsibility of the county, which maintained the road, but I wanted the executive leadership team to get a good first impression of Friar Lake, which meant I had to dispatch Juan and Rigoberto with their leaf blowers.

The exterior windows of the gatehouse needed a good scrub, but the rest of the building looked fine, from the stone threshold to the sloped tile roof. The guys had done a good job cleaning the chapel the day before; the wood rails gleamed with polish, the floors were dust-free, and daylight streamed through the stained-glass windows.

The hedge around the dormitories needed to be trimmed, and the reception area inside, where a clerk sat when we had folks in residence, smelled too much like ammonia. I checked the wall-mounted air fresheners and discovered that most of them had run out. I made a note to check for new ones in Joey's stash and get them installed.

There were at least a dozen items on my to-do list by the time Joey arrived, though they were all minor, and things that crept up on you when you were busy with bigger issues. He showed up as I was finishing my lunch out at one of the picnic tables, Rochester by my side waiting for roast beef tidbits. He was torn between food and Joey, but eventually broke away from me and romped over to Joey.

"That's a good boy," Joey said, scratching behind his ears. "You smell your buddy Brody on me? We'll have to get you guys together for a play date soon."

Joey looked better than he had the day before – he was wearing an Eastern polo shirt, with the rising sun logo on the breast, and the dark circles under his eyes were lighter. But as we got into the details of what had to be done for Friday, his stress popped up again.

"These are all quick fixes," I said. "I already sent Juan and Rigoberto out to the road to blow the leaves, and they should be done soon."

"Yeah, they were about halfway up the road when I came in."

"Let's see what you and I can accomplish ourselves, and while we're doing that you can look around for anything else that needs to be done."

We replaced the air fresheners and a dead light bulb in one of the classrooms and walked through each of the buildings. Joey had a keener eye than I did, and he found a few more things to fix or replace.

During that walk, Juan and Rigoberto returned from leaf-blowing and we set them to trimming hedges and general clean up. By the time Joey and I were ready to leave at four o'clock, the only things that remained were a couple of small items I could get done the next morning before the bigwigs arrived.

"I should be here too," Joey said. "In case Walter wants to walk around or talk to me after the meeting."

"What time is your dad's surgery?"

"They're taking him in for prep at seven-thirty," he said. "My mom and my brothers and I will be there then, and my brothers are going to leave for work as soon as he goes into surgery. The doctor says they won't get started until nine at the earliest, and the operation should take between four and six hours."

"That's good. You can come up here after they take him in, and then leave as soon as the lunch is over and Walter is done with you."

"I hate the thought of leaving my mom there all alone," Joey said.

"The truth is that neither of you can do anything. Can Mark go over and sit with her for a while?"

"He doesn't open the store until noon, so I guess he can stay with her. And my sister-in-law Becky could go over for a while until she has to pick the kids up from school."

"See, you can manage. And the most important thing will be to be there when he wakes up from the surgery. He'll be in the ICU, right? So I'm sure they have limited visiting hours. Once he's awake and resting you can spend time with him over the weekend."

After Joey left to return to the hospital, I got a text from Rick asking if I was free to meet him at our favorite hangout, the Drunken Hessian, a bar in the center of Stewart's Crossing.

I replied with the word yes and a couple of beer mug emoticons. I did some more paperwork, then shut down the computer and hurried home so that I could feed and walk Rochester before meeting Rick at the Drunken Hessian. Lili was out at photography exhibition in New Hope, so I left the dog alone, with such a big collection of bones and chew toys that it looked like a pet store threw up in my living room.

The Drunken Hessian was a bar slash tourist trap in the center of town. A plaque outside said that an inn of some kind had been on that spot since the Revolutionary War, and the décor hadn't much changed, except for the introduction of indoor plumbing. The sign depicted one of the Hessian soldiers whom Washington had surprised at Trenton on Christmas day, looking like he'd had quite a few too many.

It was a two-story building painted white, with dark green shutters. Small windows indicated rooms on the upper floor that had once been rented out but were now used for storage. In warm weather you could sit on the broad front porch and watch the traffic trickle by on Main Street.

I met Rick in the parking lot and we walked in together. He looked like he hadn't been getting much sleep, and I felt guilty that I'd woken him up the day before and essentially shoved the case on to his plate. "If I hadn't called you, would you still have gotten the murder case?" I asked. "Or would it have gone to Jerry?"

"I was up next on the roster. The call from dispatch came in about five minutes after your call, but at least I was awake then and could sound coherent."

We walked into the dim bar, past the sign that read "Suit Yourself and Seat Yourself." We picked up a couple of plastic menus, though we already knew what we were going to order, and chose a booth toward the back. The server, a skinny kid in a red and blue Hawaiian shirt and pink shorts, hustled over to us. "Dogfish Head Amber Ale, no glass," I said. "Ham cheeseburger, medium rare, with fries."

"Ditto on the beer, but I'll have bacon on my cheeseburger, and I don't want to see any blood."

"Medium well, then," the server said. "Back with your beers in a minute."

"Too much blood in your daily life?" I asked.

"I grew up on McDonalds burgers. They come one way – done." He sat back against the tall wooden booth. "You get any ideas from that website?"

"A couple," I said. He pulled out his leather-bound notebook and I told him about Drew Greenbaum and the lien against his mother's house. "I can't make a connection that killing Todd would help Drew, but he was really angry when he left the design committee meeting."

"Anger is always a good motivation," Rick said.

The server brought our beers. "I'm still going through all the material from Hi Neighbor, but I found one direct threat against Todd, from a guy named Zane Spahr."

"Spell it?"

I did. "His wife complained to Todd about potholes in the street, and one day she was out power walking, stumbled over one and fractured her tibia. Her husband says it's all Todd's fault, that he should have fixed those potholes as soon as she notified him."

"Not a very happy place, your River Bend," Rick said. "Makes me glad I don't live in a homeowner's association."

Rick had bought his parents' home when they retired to Florida, in a neighborhood near the one where I had grown up. The houses there were fifty or sixty years old, split levels and ranches, with established landscaping, perfect for families. Tamsen, on the other hand, lived in a newer development in the hills outside town. "Is there an HOA where Tamsen lives?"

He shook his head. "There's a movement to start one, so they can build a wall around the community and put up a guard gate at the entrance. With all the petty crime going on in town right now it's gaining momentum, though I don't think it will do any good. And it'll create a whole level of hassle nobody needs."

The server brought our burgers. I sliced mine in half so that it was less likely to fall apart on me and was pleased to see it was just how I liked it, a rich pink in the middle.

"Can the medical examiner narrow down the time of death?"

"Closer. Between nine PM and midnight."

We ate in silence for a minute or two. "Do you know anything about the weapon?"

"A knife with a smooth edge, not serrated. Blade at least five inches long."

"I have a knife that I inherited from my father," I said. "It's about the right length and has a sharp blade. It fits in a leather holster that snaps on to my belt."

"And you carry this?"

I shook my head. "It's in a drawer in my bedroom. Last time I used it was to cut some branches that sprawled over into the courtyard." I picked up my burger again. "The point is that it's not that uncommon to have a knife like that, and a guy could carry it on his belt, you know, in case he ever needs to use it."

Rick looked at me. "For what purpose?"

"Rochester has gotten his leash tangled in bushes a couple of times, and I've had to break the branch to get him loose. You get a pebble in your shoe, a knife blade is a good way to get it out. I could list you a half dozen other reasons."

"I'll trust you on that."

We finished up and Rick told me he'd investigate Drew Greenbaum, and Zane Spahr. "And I'll keep looking through Hi Neighbor."

"Seems like the site ought to be called Goodbye Neighbor," he said.

"I'll send them a message about it."

10: The Way the World Works

Friday morning I took Rochester out at dawn. Maybe it was just the turns we took, but the neighborhood looked much friendlier than it had two days before. Intermittent streetlights were still on along the curving streets of River Bend. Many houses had installed small solar lights along driveways and leading up to front doors – which I was sure the design committee would object to, even though I thought they were nice.

Then we turned a corner to discover one of those lights shattered on the street in front of a house on Bratislava Place, and I had to pull Rochester away so he didn't get glass in his paws. I realized that bulb and its casing had been on the street for a couple of days. Why hadn't the maintenance man who rode around in a golf cart emptying the dog waste cans and picking up tree branches cleaned that up? Or the person or family that lived in the house?

Maybe there was a point to restricting some elements of home design, if people weren't going to clean up their own problems. Not signs like mine, though.

On every block it seemed a father in business suit or a mother in sweatpants and T-shirt was hurrying sleepy-eyed kids into the car. The public-school bus picked up kids at either end of River Bend, so parents often drove their kids the couple of blocks to the exit, or even to local private schools like the George School in Newtown.

When I was a kid there were no gated communities, and the school bus traveled through The Lakes, the neighborhood where I'd grown up. The bus stop was around the corner from our house, so in winter I'd stay inside until I saw it lumbering down the street, then make a last-minute dash to the stop to hop on.

My father thought that was the ultimate in laziness. He had grown up in Newark, and it cost a nickel to ride the streetcar to his high school. He almost always walked, to save the nickel. And the snow was a lot higher back then, and life was harder.

Yeah, I remembered the stories. But I would have no kids to repeat those stories to, or to tell stories of my own.

When I got to Friar Lake at nine, Rigoberto and Juan were already hard at work. Juan swept the front steps of the chapel, while Rigoberto ran the leaf blower through the parking lot one last time.

Rochester and I walked the whole property, looking for last minute problems, and then at ten o'clock the caterers arrived. I let them in the rear of the chapel and showed them around the kitchen. We'd used the same company for the past year, but they had a high turnover rate, so the staff was always new.

They'd forgotten an extension cord, so I had to get them one from Joey's office. I was running all around the property until eleven-thirty, when President Babson's secretary Cecilia Sanchez pulled up in her vintage Ford Mustang. She was a charming Venezuelan woman who ruled Babson's office with a velvet glove over an iron hand.

"How's everything going?" she asked, after we'd said hello.

"All in hand." I'd banished Juan and Rigoberto to the rear of the property, where they could trim some of the trees that bordered on the nature preserve – keeping busy but not interfering with the event.

Joey rushed past us in his truck as we walked up to the chapel. Cecilia raised a well-trimmed eyebrow but said nothing, and I walked her through all our preparations. The next hour moved quickly as members of the board of directors and the executive council arrived. President Babson stood on the steps of the chapel greeting everyone with handshakes and hugs.

He had aged since I first returned to Eastern some five years before, but it I couldn't see it. His jet-black hair showed no signs of gray, and he worked the crowd with the enthusiasm of a man twenty years younger. I had heard rumors that he might retire when he reached sixty-five, in a year or so, but I doubted it. He lived and breathed our very good small college, and I couldn't imagine him doing anything other than running it.

Walter Gibbs arrived in the middle of the crowd. He was a tall man with ebony skin, gray streaks in his black hair, and a slight stoop. I noticed the way he stood by his car surveying the property and hoped he wouldn't find anything to complain to Joey about.

I hadn't been invited to the meeting, or the lunch following, so I stayed in the kitchen, where I could eavesdrop. Babson gave an eloquent speech about the state of the college, citing rising average SAT scores and the percentage of students who had been valedictorians or salutatorians at their high schools.

"We are also increasing the representation of students who are the first in their family to go to college," he said. "As you may know, we tread a delicate line in our attempts to achieve diversity in our student body. We will never set racial quotas or give preferential treatment to any minority group, but by focusing on those who need our help to become successful college students, we feel we are achieving our diversity goals."

That was a clever work-around. Sure, there were white students who were the first in their families to go to college, many of them children of immigrants. But it was also a way to give an extra boost to minority students without favoring them because of their race.

"We have added some language to our non-discrimination statement as well." He looked down at the paper in front of him and read, "Eastern College does not discriminate on the basis of race, color, ethnicity, genetic information, national origin, marital status, sex, disability, or age in its programs or activities."

One of the board members, an older woman with a blonde bouffant whose family owned the biggest car dealership in the Delaware Valley, raised her hand. "What does that mean, genetic information?"

I could see Babson trying to figure out how to answer that while remaining politically correct. Cecilia stood up and walked over to him and handed him her phone. He peered down at it. "Ah yes, here's the government regulation. I'm quoting here. The Genetic Information Nondiscrimination Act of 2008, also referred to as GINA, is a federal law that protects Americans from being treated unfairly because of differences in their DNA that may affect their health. The law prevents discrimination from health insurers and employers."

He handed the phone back to Cecilia, who returned to her place. "What that means in a nutshell is that we've always had people among us who feel that they were born into the wrong gender, but now they feel more comfortable expressing that concern and taking steps to become more comfortable in who they are."

He leaned forward. I'd always believed he had students' best interest at heart, no matter what he did, and I admired him for that. "We are also seeing a trend in our students toward gender non-conformity—young women who prefer to wear men's clothes, for example, without specifically making a statement about their sexual orientation. We want all those people, our students, faculty and staff, to feel comfortable at Eastern."

Walter Gibbs raised his hand then, and Babson called on him. "The issue of bathroom use has gotten a lot of press lately, and as a result, I've initiated a survey of all restroom facilities in college buildings. We'll shortly be preparing a brochure indicating the location of all single-use restroom facilities so that everyone can feel comfortable using them."

I was proud that Eastern was so forward-thinking, though I could see the blonde woman didn't seem happy with Babson's response.

After the meeting finished, we opened the screens and invited everyone to lunch. I remained in the kitchen, watching nervously as the servers delivered and removed plates, but no plates were dropped, no glasses spilled.

As the attendees finished their desserts and began to leave, Cecilia came into the kitchen. "President Babson asked me to tell you he'd like to speak with you before he leaves. Can you come with me?"

I followed her, and we lingered in the background while Babson finished an intense conversation with the trustee in the blonde bouffant. His body language was intense and yet personal, respecting her space yet leaning forward so that she was the total focus of his attention. By the time he was finished she was smiling and nodding, and he clasped her hand in both of his and smiled.

When she walked off he turned to me, and Cecilia faded into the background. "I'm pleased with the job you're doing, Steve," he said. "But you know, colleges and universities are getting their funds cut right and left these days. This new initiative to bring in first-time in college students has been much more expensive than expected."

My heart began to thump. Was he going to close Friar Lake to save money?

"The bottom line is that we need to make this place a real profit center," he continued, and I took a deep breath. "We floated a bond to finance the construction, as you know, and bond interest is one of the financial areas we're looking at closely. I know it doesn't cost much to keep this place open—your salary and the other staff costs are minimal, the solar panels are working to keep our utility costs low, and we're not paying real estate tax. But I want to improve your facility utilization—what's your percentage now?"

I struggled to think of how to phrase it. "We have at least one internal or external program each week," I finally said. "Some of those last only a few hours, like today's meeting and lunch. Our longest was the two-week Upward Bound course for high school students. I'd have to put together the numbers for you."

"Do that, if you would, please." He was about my height, a shade under six feet, so his green eyes looked directly into mine. "Friar Lake is one of my pet projects and I want to make sure it outlasts my tenure here."

Then he shook my hand and turned to follow Cecilia to his car. I wanted to call out to him to wait—what did that mean about his tenure? Was he planning to leave Eastern soon? What kind of utilization rate was he looking for?

But he was gone. Across from me I saw Joey deep in conversation with Walter Gibbs, and I walked back to the kitchen, where one of the servers had put together a plate of leftovers for Rochester. I walked back toward my office, where I'd left the hound with a bowl of water and a selection of chew toys. He was a friendly dog, but way too friendly for a formal event like the one just ended.

I snuck around to the side of the gatehouse and peered in the window. He was sprawled on the floor, sound asleep, three different rawhide bones in easy reach of his mouth.

When I walked in the front door, though, he was already there, with a mournful look on his face like he thought I'd abandoned him and was never coming back.

"Don't worry, I brought something for you," I said, holding up the white paper bag, which contained a foil package of lunchtime leftovers wrapped like a swan. I sat in my office chair and fed him tidbits of turkey by hand to keep him from scarfing everything all at once. I had finished and was in the rest room washing my hands when Joey came in.

"How did your meeting with Walter go?" I asked as I stepped

out, drying my hands on a paper towel.

"Better than I expected, and worse." Joey collapsed onto the Windsor armchair across from my desk, the one with the Eastern rising sun crest on the back splat, and Rochester came over to nuzzle him.

"Walter says I'm doing such a great job here that he could use my help on some work on the campus," Joey said, as he scratched behind Rochester's ears.

"That's good."

"Yeah, but the timing is bad. With my dad in the hospital I can barely keep up with what's going on here. And even when he gets home, my mom will need some extra help with him for a while. My brothers are trying, but they're busy too, and I can't keep relying on Mark."

"I'm sure he won't mind."

"I know, that's his personality. He loves my parents, but the point is they're my parents, not his, so I need to bear the brunt of the burden."

"What does Walter need you to do on campus?" I asked.

"It's about this bathroom survey."

"Oh, yeah, I heard him mention that during Babson's speech. Identifying all the single-use bathrooms on campus, right?"

Joey nodded. "Walter had one of his work-study students do the legwork, walking around the campus and checking each building's bathroom and marking it on the plans. But he discovered the kid didn't really know what he was doing. He marked places on the plans that don't have a restroom at all, and he got confused about which ones had urinals and which ones didn't."

He slumped back against the chair. "Now the whole thing needs to be done again and he wants me to do it."

"I don't mind spending time on campus. We can split up the buildings between us."

"Are you sure? If you can handle the survey part, I can take what you give me and check the information against the plans. But don't you have work to do here?"

"Babson wants me to give him up to date numbers on facility utilization," I said. "And once that's done, he wants to increase the revenue we generate so we can pay down the renovation bond quicker."

"At least he's not thinking about shutting the place down."

"Not yet, at least. He agrees we're doing a good job staying within our budget, but someday that might not be enough. He wants us to be a real profit center for the college."

"And if you can't?"

"Then he'll either find somebody who can, or shut us down," I said. "That's the way the business world works."

11: Memories

Joey and I were hashing out the details of which buildings I'd check on the campus when his cell phone rang with the first few bars of ABBA's "Mamma Mia."

"Mark set up these rings tones for me," he said, as he grabbed for the phone. "That's my mom."

He put the phone up to his ear. "Hey, mom. How's dad doing?" He listened for a moment. "Mom. The doctor said four to six hours for the surgery. It's only been four and a half since he went in. There's nothing to get frightened about."

He listened again. "Fine. I'll be over there as soon as I can." He ended the call. "My mom is freaking out. Nobody will tell her what's going on in the operating room."

"You go. I'll finish up here."

After he left, I sat in my chair, with Rochester at my knee. I'd never thought through the specifics of my mother's final illness. She'd been feeling somewhat listless, but both she and my father had dismissed it because she was unhappy at work. She was the office manager for a dental practice in Trenton, across the river from Stewart's Crossing, and the business was going through a lot of changes. The woman my mom had been with for a dozen years had retired and sold her practice to a young man, who was making a lot of changes. Many patients had moved on, and finances were tight.

She and my father finally decided she should retire. Before

she lost her health insurance, she'd gone in for a comprehensive checkup, and the doctor had ordered an ultrasound, which revealed growths on her thyroid. A biopsy showed cancer there, and further tests indicated the cancer had spread to her bones and other organs.

My father wanted to retire then, to look after her, but as she got worse she had to leave her job and they needed his insurance to cover her. Mary was pregnant for the first time, suffering a lot of morning sickness, and I had been reluctant to leave her alone to fly back to Pennsylvania and help them out. My father had to wait for my mom's surgery results on his own, and he had to negotiate the complicated insurance requirements. I had talked to them both on the phone a lot, but that wasn't the same.

She had been responding to the chemotherapy, but then she caught a chest cold which worsened into an infection, and that was the last straw. I had flown home for the funeral, of course, and a few days after I returned to California Mary had suffered her first miscarriage.

The doctor tried to comfort us, telling it was nature's way of handling a fetus that was too ill to survive, but on top of my mother's death, that was a real punch to the gut, and Mary and I both retreated into ourselves. I barely noticed all the packages coming into the house from Amazon and other online vendors, and it wasn't until I saw the first set of credit card bills that I realized how much trouble we were in.

I stroked the soft fur of Rochester's golden head and let myself cry for a few minutes, for all that I'd lost, and for the pain Joey and his family were going through. Then I wiped my eyes, took a deep breath, and stood up. I had work to do, and Joey, and perhaps even my own career, depended on me to get it done.

The rest of the day passed in a blur as I handled Joey's problems and managed to get a few minutes to think about how I could increase the number of events we handled at Friar Lake. I had already done everything that was within my comfort zone and my experience, so it was time for some new thinking. I spent an hour brainstorming, making notes and doing some quick research.

I texted Joey to check on his dad, and he replied that Joe Senior had come through the surgery without complications, but he would be in the cardiac ICU for a couple of days for follow up. I replied with a happy face and a thumbs up.

That evening, Lili and I sat together at dinner and talked about our days, and I told her about Joe Capodilupo's surgery, and the meeting and lunch at Friar Lake. "I'm glad Joe is doing well," she said. She had met Joe a couple of times in the past, both in his old job, and at a big party Joey and Mark had celebrated the year before. "It must be tough on Joey right now. I know that every time my mom gets sick, I get very stressed."

Lili's widowed mother lived in an oceanfront condo in Miami, and though she was in good health, she was closing in on her seventy-fifth birthday, with all the problems that aging brings. She had a fiery personality, which I saw echoes of in her daughter, and so even small things tended to be magnified.

Lili took a sip of the fresh apple cider we'd bought at a local orchard the weekend before, then said, "What are you going to do to bring in more programs at Friar Lake?"

"I wish I knew. I think I've maxed out the capacity for my own programming—there's a limit to the number of alumni events we can offer before we burn out the faculty and overwhelm the alums. And our market is pretty much local, so we're restricted to the graduates who still live within driving distance of the campus."

She nodded. "What about doing some different kind of programs—art exhibits, for example? I could get together some of my student work and we could hang it in the chapel."

My heart skipped a beat. What a great idea. Why didn't I think of it? "That's great—it uses the facility and it exposes more people to Friar Lake."

Then I realized the problem. "Too bad it doesn't bring in

revenue."

"Oh. That." Lili thought for a moment. "I know a guy who runs a gallery in Washington's Crossing. What if I got him to co-sponsor the event, and bring in some of his artists? He'd pay you something for the use of the space, and maybe even a small commission if he sells anything."

"That's awesome, sweetheart." I leaned across and kissed her. "I was thinking I could reach out to community groups and get them to run events there." We brainstormed a couple of ideas— clubs like the Lions and the Kiwanis did monthly lunches, so maybe we could lure them there, but Friar Lake wasn't the most convenient location for midday business. I pulled out my laptop and we started searching for organizations that met on Saturdays or Sundays.

When we had a solid list, we settled down on the couch to watch a movie together. I pushed aside all my problems, giving my subconscious a chance to come up with some ideas.

Saturday morning dawned crisp and sunny. "How would you feel about doing some apple picking?" Lili asked. "The place where I bought the cider last week has a big orchard, and Tamsen forwarded me a recipe for a sour cream apple pie that she says is terrific."

"You want to call her and see if she and Rick and Justin want to join us?"

"That's a great idea."

I went upstairs to shower and dress, and by the time I returned Lili said, "Justin and Rick have Pop Warner football practice this afternoon, but they can go with us if we go now."

Lili grabbed a light sweater and struggled to put her exuberant auburn curls under a ball cap. "I'm tired of my hair," she said. "What would you think if I got it cut?"

"I'd think you're beautiful no matter what you do with your hair."

She leaned over and kissed my cheek. "Good answer. I might go to New York one day. I saw Andrea del Presto from the sociology department the other day and her hair looked gorgeous. She has it done at a salon on Madison Avenue."

I didn't say that sounded expensive, though it did. Lili and I kept our finances separate, though we mixed and mingled expenses as they came up. My father had left me the townhouse free and clear, and Lili paid the monthly association fee. I paid the cable bill, and we each paid for our own cell phones. We alternated paying for groceries and dining out. So Lili was free to spend as much as she wanted for a hair salon, though privately I thought the discount salon in Levittown where I got my hair cut was just fine.

Tamsen picked us up a half hour later in her SUV, which was the only vehicle among us that could accommodate all five of us and the two dogs easily. She was accustomed to chauffeuring kids to all kinds of after-school activities, from sports to carnivals to library enrichment events.

Justin and Rascal were already in the back, so we opened the hatch and Rochester jumped in with them. The two dogs were clambering over Justin as Lili and I slipped into the back seat, the boy giggling with joy as they licked his face and squirmed around him.

Tamsen drove us inland, up Ferry Road. On the way, we passed a truck advertising Female Plumbing, with a sign on the right that read, "It takes a woman to get the job done right."

I pointed the truck out to Lili and Tamsen. "Would you guys really consider going to an ob-gyn who advertised herself as a female plumber?" I asked them both.

"Steve. They're plumbers who happen to be women," Lili said. "Not ob-gyns."

I leaned forward. "Oh."

Tamsen, Lili and even Rick laughed at me.

"What's an obie gin?" Justin asked from the back.

Rick turned around and looked at me. "You brought it up."

I turned toward Justin. "A doctor for moms," I said. "To make sure they can take care of their kids."

"Do you have good one, Mom?" Justin asked.

"I have a great doctor, and a great kid," Tamsen answered. "What do you want to do when we get to Styer's? Should we pick the apples ourselves or just buy a bushel?"

I admired the way she was able segue so smoothly. I wondered briefly if Mary, who had remarried and now had a child, had developed those same skills. I'd never know.

"I want to pick the apples," Justin said. "Do you think I can reach them?"

"I'll pull the branches down for you, sport," Rick said.

We drove what had once been country roads, now four-lane divided highways, out to the outskirts of Langhorne, where Styer Orchards was one of the only farms to have held out against suburban encroachment. A sign out front proclaimed that the land had been preserved as a working orchard, which I assumed meant some kind of government subsidy was involved.

We passed an old-fashioned tractor outside the entrance to the market and followed a sign down the road to the orchard. We skipped the pumpkin patch and headed for the orchard, where we got a couple of baskets and walked between the rows of the trees to where the apples were ripe.

The air was fresh with the smells of dirt and apple bark, and the dogs romped around us, though we held them on leashes. When we got to the right spot, Lili and Tamsen took the leashes and settled down on a grassy spot to watch Rick, Justin and me pick the apples. Rick and I took turns pulling branches down for Justin, while loading the basket ourselves.

It was an idyllic way to pass a Saturday morning. The trees

were bowed with fruit, the pathways neat and well-kept, and around us we saw other families doing the same thing we were.

"Lili has promised me a sour cream apple pie," I said to Rick as we worked.

"Tamsen has the recipe," Rick said. He turned to Justin. "You like apple pie, sport?"

"I love it. Especially if my mom makes it."

Rick laughed. "This kid's going to grow up to be a diplomat."

"I want to be a football coach," Justin said. "Like you."

I smiled. My parents used to take me to Styer's when I was a kid. I learned quickly that my mother didn't want me to eat candy apples, worried about cavities, but my dad was an easy mark. All I had to do was take him by the hand and lead him to them, and he'd buy one for each of us. I hoped Justin would have similar good memories.

He rushed ahead to his mom, leaving Rick and me to carry baskets brimming with ripe Braeburn apples in shades of pink and pale green, which Tamsen had informed us made the best pies.

"Anything new on the murder case?" I asked Rick as we walked.

"I have a series of interviews set up for Monday and Tuesday," he said. "At this point I'm still gathering information, and the chief isn't eager to pay for overtime unless I can prove the need. You find anything more on the Hi Neighbor site?"

"Honestly, I haven't looked. My boss gave me a directive yesterday afternoon that freaked me out, that I need to increase the revenue at Friar Lake, and I've been focused on that."

When we returned to the farm stand with our baskets, I noticed that a woman in a pretty flowered apron was giving a lesson on how to make baked apples. I looked at Lili and knew she had the same thought. "You have a kitchen at Friar Lake," she said.

"It's not quite set up for lessons, but I bet we could manage," I said. "Great minds think alike."

We bought a big pumpkin for our yard, and a sheaf of Indian corn for the front door, as well as our apples, and I bought red delicious candy apples for Rick, Justin and myself that glowed with a tooth-cracking sheen. I would have bought for Lili and Tamsen, too, but they declined, Tamsen because she had to drive, and Lili because she found them too sweet.

Well, she'd have to have other memories of us, then.

12: High Five

When I took Rochester out for his walk that afternoon, just before dusk, a few clouds were gray smudges against the light blue canopy of the sky. On Minsk Court, we passed a young mom with an infant in a stroller and a boy of four or five on foot. I'd spoken to her before, because the boy got excited whenever he saw a dog. He was not even as tall as my golden, but he was fearless in his approach.

He cried, "Yay!" and Rochester pulled us toward him. The boy's mom, on the phone, tried to rein him in, without success, but it didn't matter, because Rochester met him halfway. The boy grabbed a hunk of Rochester's fur and kissed him on the side of his head.

I knelt to his level and took his hand gently in mine. "Let me show you the best way to come up to a dog." I held out his palm for Rochester to sniff, and then lick, and the boy giggled.

"See, that way the dog gets to know you. Otherwise he might get scared by a big, strong boy like you."

I heard the mom finish her call. "Sorry, I have to go. I'll work on finding a location for the meeting, I promise."

I stood up. "I hope you don't mind that I spoke to your son," I said. "But you know there are some dogs in the community that get skittish when someone rushes up to them."

"Oh, no, I appreciate it," she said. "I'm Epiphania Kosta, and this is Giorgios, and his brother in the stroller is Alexander."

"*Yassou*," I said, remembering to accent the first syllable, the way I'd been taught.

"You speak Greek?" she asked.

"Just a couple of words. My next-door-neighbors growing up were Greek. I figured with a name like Epiphania you had to be Greek. I'm Steve, by the way."

We shook hands. "You figured right. Named for my grandmother. I could have been a Helen or a Diana, like my sisters, but I was first born."

I decided to embrace my run of luck in coming up with ideas for Friar Lake. And maybe Rochester had tugged me over there because he had a sixth sense Epiphania could be helpful to me. I'd learned to trust his instincts.

"I couldn't help overhearing you were looking for a meeting place," I said. "I run a conference center for Eastern College, upriver just north of Bowman's Tower, and we host events there all the time."

"We do have a kind of educational mission," she said, considering.

"What's your group?"

"The La Leche League. We encourage women to breast feed, and we have regular meeting with speakers who talk about the benefits of human milk for babies."

"Does our location work for you?"

"Sure. We have members all the way from Bristol to Easton, so somewhere halfway between would be terrific. Do you have a card?"

I shook my head. "Never think of bringing them when I walk. But I have my phone—can you share your contact with me?"

It was easier for her to just call me, and then after I ended the call we each created a contact on our respective phones. "I'll email you a package that includes all the details," I said. Then I squatted down to Giorgios, who was busy examining a stone on the pavement. "Can you show me what you learned today?"

He looked up and nodded eagerly and held his hand out to Rochester the way I'd showed him. "Good job, dude." I high-fived him, getting some of Rochester's saliva on my palm, and then we turned for home.

"That was sweet," I said to Rochester as we walked. "I hope that'll work out."

§ § § §

Sunday morning Rochester woke up at the same time as every day for his walk, but at least because it was Sunday I could stumble back into bed for another hour. After a breakfast of bagels, lox and cream cheese, Lili delegated me to start peeling and slicing apples so she could get to work on the sour cream apple pie recipe Tamsen had given her.

"You've never been much of a baker," I commented, as we worked. "Did your mom bake?"

Lili shook her head. "She wasn't big on desserts. She'd bake us cakes for our birthdays because it was an American custom, but they weren't very good. When my father wasn't traveling for work, he'd buy us the kind of Jewish desserts he grew up with – strudel and black and white cookies and rugelach. He made a big deal of finding us hamantashen for Purim wherever we were."

She looked up. "My mom used to criticize his sweet tooth and complain that he was going to make us fat."

"Your mom certainly had some charming moments," I said. "My mother's mother was a terrific baker and my mom always said she didn't want to compete. And then after my Nana died my mother claimed not to have any of her recipes."

We worked smoothly together until the pie was in the oven. Then we took Rochester down to a mini-park by the Delaware and let him run loose, though instead of romping through the piles of autumn leaves he wanted to pee on each one.

I had to leave for Friar Lake soon after that. Though it was a Sunday, we'd arranged with a community soccer team from Washington's Crossing to practice drills on one of our hillside fields. We weren't charging them anything, but the event met one of the criteria President Babson had established when we opened the center, that we serve the neighboring community. Joey and I usually alternated weekend duty, taking comp time during the week in exchange, and even if his father hadn't been sick, it was my turn.

Between drills, I chatted up the coach, who ran an interior design store in the center of town and who might be interested in running a series of design workshops. I was proud of myself that I was pushing forward on any idea.

After they left, Rochester and I did a quick run around the area to make sure none of the kids had left any gear behind. That is, I looked around, and he settled by a tree to chew something. When I finished I tried to call him, but he wouldn't come. I had to walk over and pry his jaws open.

At first, I was horrified—it looked like he was chewing part of someone's mouth. Then I realized it was a kid's dental retainer, a plastic horseshoe with the imprint of teeth all around it. "Yuck," I said, as I held it with the tip of two fingers. "You find the grossest stuff to chew, dog."

On our way home, I called the soccer coach and let him know that I'd found a retainer, and he said he'd check with his kids to see who might have lost one.

After dinner, Lili served up slices of the pie. It was terrific, the crust flaky, the apples meltingly tender, the sour cream and walnut topping a perfect accompaniment. "Tamsen and I promised each other we would put aside a piece so we could taste-test both of them."

"Why would you want to compete like that?" I asked.

She just looked at me and shook her head.

As Lili and I were cleaning up, my phone blipped with a text from Mark Figueroa, Joey Capodilupo's partner. "I'm worried about Joey," he wrote. "He's so stressed between his dad and his job. Can you help?"

I texted back and agreed to meet Mark the next morning at the Chocolate Ear, which was only a few blocks from his antique store, though I warned him I needed to get to Friar Lake early to make sure Joey's guys were doing their work.

Monday morning had all the hallmarks of a glorious Indian summer day. Sunshine glimmered off the morning dew resting on the last of the petunia blossoms in window boxes along Main Street. There was a pleasant chill in the air, but it wasn't too cold to sit outside.

I tied Rochester's leash around the base of one of the wrought-iron tables. I went inside, where the walls were painted a mellow yellow and decorated with Art Deco posters of French food products like Gautier cognac and Chocolat Carpentier. I ordered a hot chocolate and a ham and cheese croissant for breakfast. Gail baked special dog biscuits, shaped like a bone and iced in pretty colors, and I bought one for Rochester.

I was sipping my hot chocolate, flavored with raspberry, when Mark Figueroa came hurrying down the sidewalk. He was a tall guy, nearly six-six, and when I first met him he'd been scarecrow-skinny. Since living with Joey, he'd filled out a bit, though his polo shirt was still loose on him and his jeans barely reached to the tops of his loafers. His hair dark was tousled, and he looked like he'd just woken up.

"Sorry I'm late," he said. "Joey's been with his parents and I had to do all the Brody care this morning." Brody was their pure-white golden retriever, and he was a handful. Even Rochester had trouble keeping him in line.

"No worries," I said, as Rochester jumped up to greet Mark and sniff for traces of Brody. "The hound and I are enjoying the

Indian summer sun."

After letting Rochester sniff his legs and his hand, Mark went into the café, and Rochester slumped back to the sidewalk beside me, though he was keeping his eye on a squirrel in the oak tree beside us.

Mark came out a couple of minutes later with a steaming cappuccino and a chocolate croissant. He slid into the seat across from me. "Thanks for coming to meet me. I'm getting really worried about all the stress Joey is under, at work and now with his father, and you're the only person I can think of who could help."

"What's the matter?"

"Joey has always been this easy-going, happy guy. But lately he's been very stressed, starting even before his dad got sick."

He gulped some of his coffee, then put the cup down on the saucer. "You know he got a new boss after his dad retired? Walter Gibbs?"

"Yeah." Joe Capodilupo senior had retired about six months before, replaced by an executive who'd come to us from one of the big colleges in Philadelphia. Though Joey and I were co-managers at Friar Lake, we hadn't discussed the new guy. "Has that been a problem?"

"It's hard to tell if it's all on Joey, or if it's his boss. I don't think Walter likes the fact that Joey used to work for his dad, and he's cracking down on him. Joey's been stressed about that. Lots of new forms to fill out and meetings to go to. He's in a weird position because he's the only guy with his own facility to take care of—everyone else works on the main campus."

A pickup truck boosted on huge wheels cruised slowly past us, blasting Tiffany's "I Think We're Alone Now," and I had a momentary impulse to jump up and dance the way the members of the Umbrella Academy did in what I thought was a classic sequence. But I restrained myself and focused on Mark.

"And now with this stuff with his dad," he continued, when the music trailed away. "Joey's taking off to be with his family and I'm worried Walter won't like that."

"If Joey's taking personal leave, his boss can't complain. But I understand Joey wants to do a good job. I've already been helping – I got the landscape guys going yesterday and dealt with a plumber Joey had scheduled."

"That's great, and I'm sure he appreciates it. But his parents have been on him non-stop," Mark said. "They think that because his brothers both have families they can't ask them for anything. Joey's the one who has to talk to the doctors, and run his mother around, and sit with his dad and keep him company." His body sagged. "Even though it's only been a couple of days, it's taking a toll on both of us."

"What can I do to help?"

"Can you make sure everything's going smoothly at work without him? And let him know that? That would make him feel better."

"Sure. And I know Joe Senior, so one day I can go over and sit with him for a while, give Joey a break."

Mark smiled broadly. "That would be awesome."

Too bad I couldn't take Rochester to the hospital – he was enough to cheer anybody up. I hoped I'd be able to stand in his paws.

13: Bathroom Break

I had to hustle up the River Road after I finished with Mark, because I didn't want Juan and Rigoberto to hang around too long with nothing to do. Joey had promised to be back at work Tuesday or Wednesday, depending on his dad's condition, so I reminded myself these very early mornings were only a temporary issue.

I gave Rigoberto and Juan their marching orders for the morning, then prepared for the mission I'd promised to help Joey with, counting bathrooms on the Eastern campus. I didn't want to leave Rochester alone in the gatehouse, so shortly after nine o'clock I bundled him back in the car with me. "You want to spend some time with Mama Lili?" I asked him, as I backed out of the parking space. "Just promise not to eat any of her student art projects."

That reminded me of the retainer, and I noted that the soccer coach hadn't gotten back to me.

Friar Lake wasn't far from Eastern as the crow flies, but the crow didn't lay out Bucks County's country roads. I had to do a lot of zigzagging, up and down hills, in order to arrive in Leighville, a small town of old stone and Carpenter Gothic buildings a few miles farther upriver.

Eastern College sat atop a hill that overlooked the town, leading to a few town-and-gown crises in the past, as people complained the college looked down its nose at the town.

President Babson had made some progress in that area, creating after-school programs for kids, staffed by education majors, and inviting high schoolers up to the campus for tours and seminars on applying to college and getting financial aid.

Nineteenth-century administrators eager to attach their own reputations to those who preceded them had emulated the style of Oxford and Cambridge by nineteenth century administrators eager. Therefore, most of the buildings were designed in the collegiate Gothic style, gray stone with arched doorways and crenellated towers.

Technically, only service dogs were allowed on the Eastern campus, but I'd gotten an exception for Rochester years before when Babson was eager to hire me for a project in the alumni relations department, and willing to break a rule or two on my behalf. I knew most of the college security officers, so no one ever complained.

I parked in the lot behind Granger Hall, one of the more unique structures on campus. Donated by a pharmaceutical magnate, it was designed to resemble a pill capsule, white glass on the lower half, maroon glass on the upper half, with a brown band around the fourth floor. The building housed communications and fine arts, and we walked up to Lili's second floor office on a central curving staircase, through an atrium lit by the glass dome above.

Lili's office had big windows that looked out on the campus, golden in the fall light. Most of the photos on the walls of her office were student work, though there were a couple of her own, including one of a Sudanese mother and child, their somber faces bathed in the ethereal glow of a sunbeam shooting down from a cloudy sky.

"Thanks for watching the hound," I said. Lili was behind her desk, working at her computer, and he hurried over to say hello to her.

"How long do you think you'll be? I have a meeting of all the academic deans at one o'clock."

"Why don't I plan to finish by noon and we'll have lunch at the Cafette?" I walked over and gave her a peck on the cheek.

"Sounds like a plan," she said, and returned to her work.

Granger Hall was one of the newer buildings on campus, and according to the schedule Joey had given me, all the restrooms were either designated for men or women, though there was a single "family" restroom on the first floor that was suitable for use by anyone.

I checked it out. Single toilet, sink, hand dryer and fold-down changing table. I made a note on my list that I had verified it and decided to continue with the oldest building at Eastern, Fields Hall, the Victorian stone mansion that had once been the home of Eastern's founder.

My first full-time job at Eastern had been with the alumni relations department, where I maintained the records database, pulled out groups of alums to approach for various fund-raising possibilities and updated new addresses, new jobs, and death records. My office was a small room that had been carved out of a much larger one, fortunately with big French doors that led out to the gardens, and I had great memories of working there.

I navigated the labyrinthine corridors of the repurposed mansion, saying hello to old friends and colleagues, as I surveyed each of the bathrooms. As expected, there hadn't been enough room to create big single-sex facilities, so each of the ones I checked was a single stall, though a few had urinals as well as toilets.

I found one more bathroom, on the third floor, that the work-study student had missed, and marked it on my map. I kept going, working through other older buildings on campus, until noon, when I walked over to the Cafette, an on-campus sandwich shop in an old carriage house behind Fields Hall. It was a worn, homey-looking place, with scarred wooden picnic tables and benches and the remains of a brick chimney.

I ordered for both of us, verified that the two bathrooms in the back were both single-use, and snagged a table outside, under the red and gold canopy of a spreading maple tree. A pair of students sat at a table nearby, the young woman in a crop top, shorts and cat's ear barrettes, the boy in a Philadelphia Eagles shirt and jeans. How easy life had been back then, I thought. I'd fallen in and out of love with a couple of different girls, going to on-campus movies, dances, and to hear visiting poets. I'd never considered all the complications that would come with becoming an adult.

"This is probably one of the last days we can eat outside," Lili said, as she sank into the padded wooden chair across from me. Rochester rushed up to sniff my hand and make sure it was me, then flopped on the grass beside my feet.

"Then I'm glad we get to enjoy it together." I raised my paper cup of lemonade to toast the mug of coffee I had gotten for her. Light cream, two sugars, the way she liked it.

"How'd your bathroom survey go?" she asked. "Did seeing so many of them make you need to go, and go?"

"I'm not quite that old," I said, in what I hoped was wry humor rather than irritation. "I covered about half the campus and found a couple of single-use restrooms the work study student missed. I need to get back to Friar Lake after we're finished eating, so I'll have to come back tomorrow and finish."

"I'm interviewing new adjuncts tomorrow morning, so I can't have Rochester."

"That's okay, I have to host a meeting of the faculty senate subcommittee on academic ethics tomorrow afternoon so I can't stay here too long."

"Why are they coming all the way out to Friar Lake?"

"No on-campus classrooms big enough for them at the time they need to meet," I said. "I'm glad to have them. The more faculty I can introduce to the facility the better."

"You know a meeting that big, about that contentious a topic, is going to degenerate into a shouting match, don't you?"

"Why should academic ethics be a big deal topic? We all agree plagiarism is wrong, and so is allowing students to make discriminatory comments in class. When I saw the meeting request, I figured it was just one of those issues professors like to bloviate about." Before she could argue, I held up my hand and said, "Present company excepted."

"A professor at one of those big Midwest land-grant universities got censured for refusing to give a recommendation to a student who wanted to study in Israel," she said. "The committee has been charged with developing guidelines for recommendations."

"I generally give a recommendation to any student who asks for one," I said. "Except in the case of a student I gave a D to a couple of years ago. I told him I valued my academic integrity and I couldn't write him a false letter. He couldn't understand that, and I finally had to get up and physically walk him out of the adjunct area at the English department, because he wouldn't let up."

"See, that's a case where we need a policy. Another that has come up is a professor of philosophy here at Eastern. He put all his lecture notes in a three-ring binder and he's selling them through the bookstore. A student complained, and the issue got bounced up to the committee. There are at least three more issues on the agenda that have people's fur ruffled."

"I'll have to plan to make my introduction and welcome and then duck out," I said.

14: Prayer for Health

By the time Rochester and I got back to Friar Lake, Rigoberto and Juan had finished the work I'd assigned them and were sitting under one of the big oak trees near my office. I didn't want to tell them that Rochester often peed around that tree.

"You have more work for us, *jefe*?" Rigoberto asked. I noticed he was the one who always spoke; perhaps Juan didn't speak much English.

I pulled out my phone and looked at the list Joey had texted me. I sent them off to clean the biggest classroom in preparation for the meeting the next day. I realized I had given them too little do that morning; I'd have to figure out how to avoid that in the future and keep them busy, at least until Joey came back to take over.

Epiphania called me that afternoon to discuss a meeting of the La Leche League, and I had to put together a proposal for her and send it off, and by the time I was finished I saw Juan and Rigoberto leaving in the battered sedan.

There had to be other groups out there like the League; how could I find them? I did a lot of Google searching until I stumbled on a company that offered lists of groups and organizations, sorted by zip code order. I jumped through a couple of hoops, giving them my email address, accepting their privacy policy, then waiting for a confirmation email back from them.

When I finally got access to the site, I discovered it was kind of a scam. Sure, you could get a list for free—but all it did was give you the name of the organization. If you wanted specific details, like contact person, address or phone number, you had to pay.

Normally, that wouldn't be a problem. I worked for Eastern, and I had a budget for program development. But the list was expensive, and the way they'd tricked me sat badly with me. I had a powerful urge to make a note of their URL and then go home that evening and hack into their database, taking whatever I wanted.

I took a deep breath. For the most part, I'd been able to control my impulses toward digital burglary; the threat of a return to prison was a powerful motivator. But every now and then I'd get this urge to snoop around somewhere I didn't belong.

Fortunately, the tools I used to hack were on a separate laptop back home, stowed in the attic so that I'd have to take extra steps to retrieve it. I printed out the list of group names and went to work the old-fashioned way—Googling each one individually to find the information I needed. It was dull, tedious work, but it was legal.

And that was what mattered.

§§§§

That evening, after I'd fed and walked Rochester and had dinner with Lili, I drove over to St. Mary's Hospital in Langhorne, where Joe Senior was recovering from his bypass surgery.

On my way there, I got a call from the soccer coach. The kid who had lost the retainer had a couple of them, so I could just throw away the one I had found.

Before I walked into Joe Senior's room, I glanced through the open door and saw Joey sitting by his bed. Joey was six feet tall and broad-shouldered, but in his father's hospital room he looked tired and diminished. He wore a faded plaid shirt and jeans, and as usual a backwards ball cap over his dark hair.

I walked in the room, where Joe Senior was sitting up in bed and talking animatedly with Joey. He didn't look like a guy who'd just suffered a major heart attack; his color was good, and he was smiling. If anything, he looked better than his son.

Joey's dad was shorter and stockier than he was. The dome of his head was bald, surrounded by a fringe of white like one of those old-time monks. But I saw the family resemblance in the roundness of his face, and the way his smile reached all the way up to his eyes when he saw me. Joey smiled the same way.

"Steve! What brings you over to this sorry excuse for a center of healing?" Joe asked.

"Came to check on you. Make sure you're not terrorizing the nurses."

"I've got my boy here to keep tabs on me," Joe said. He looked from me to Joey. "Let me guess. Mark sent you over? He's worried about Joey, isn't he?"

"Should he be?" I asked, looking at both of them.

"He needs to get more sleep," Joe said. "When he was a teenager you had to get a forklift to force him out of bed. Of my three boys Joey was the one who slept the most." He shook his head. "Now he's here all the time. I tell him to go home, but he doesn't listen."

"Mom needs a break now and then."

"Why don't I stay here and keep your dad company for a while, and you go home," I said to Joey. "Visiting hours end at nine anyway. I'll stick around until then."

"You don't have to do that," Joey said.

"What? You worried we'll talk about you?" his father said. "Go on, get out of here, you big bum."

I could see the uncertainty on Joey's face, but finally he stood up. He leaned down and kissed his father's forehead. "Take care, Pop. I'll see you in the morning."

Joey reached out to shake my hand, but I pulled him into

an embrace. "Take care of yourself," I said. "You're no good to anybody if you let yourself get run down."

"Yeah, that's what Mark says."

He took one more look at his father, the way Orpheus couldn't resist looking back at Eurydice, and then he walked out. I sat down beside Joe in the surprisingly comfortable armchair and looked around at the single room. It was painted a pale green, with a big framed photograph of a Bucks County barn along the side wall. Across from Joe's bed was a whiteboard with the day and date, as well as the name of his nurse and his CNA, or certified nursing assistant.

Joe was wired up to a monitor that beeped softly as it tracked his heart rate, the lines spiking up and down in a regular pattern. "I'm glad you came over, Steve," Joe said. "How's my boy doing at Friar Lake? He won't tell me anything."

"The property's running like a well-oiled clock. You and he did a great job with the renovation, so there haven't been any big problems." I rapped on my head. "Knock on wood."

"And Walter Gibbs, the guy who replaced me?"

"I've only met him once, briefly, on Friday."

"Steve. I have three sons. I know when somebody's hiding something. Spill it."

I shrugged. "Just what Mark said. That Gibbs has a lot of new forms and procedures, and he's coming down hard on Joey."

"Lousy time for me to get sick. I hate to pull Joey away from work, but my other boys don't have such flexible jobs, and they've got wives and families to look out for."

"I'll keep a handle on things at Friar Lake while Joey's out," I said. "Don't worry about that."

We segued into conversation about mutual friends and acquaintances from Eastern, where Joe had spent the bulk of his career. I didn't realize it was nine o'clock until a nurse came in and told me I had to go.

I wished Joe well and a quick recovery from his bypass surgery and promised once more that I'd look after Joey at Friar Lake. If the physical plant started to show signs of neglect, that would reflect poorly on him, and perhaps even on me. I needed to make sure that didn't happen.

§§§§

Tuesday morning I drove up the winding road to Friar Lake right behind Juan and Rigoberto, and I gave them a list of chores that ought to carry them all the way through the day. Then I left Rochester in my office and went over to Eastern to finish my bathroom survey.

It wasn't even eight o'clock yet, and the campus was still in an early-morning slumber. The sun glittered on dew on the undisturbed lawns, and only a few eager students hurried along the flagstone paths from dorms to classroom buildings.

The ability to create your own schedule was a revelation to me when I landed at Eastern. Pennsbury High classes began at 7:45 AM, and I had to catch my bus at seven. I struggled to drag my teenage carcass out of bed in time to pull on my clothes, down a glass of orange juice and a couple of brown sugar and cinnamon pop-tarts, grab my backpack and run out to the bus.

At Eastern, my first class was at ten AM, and all I had to was get up early enough to hit the dining hall for breakfast beforehand. I was only in class for twelve hours a week, leaving me plenty of time for playing club tennis, taking a yoga class in one of the dance studios, and putting in ten hours at my work-study job.

There was homework, too, but reading books for my English classes never seemed like work. I went to every class, paid attention and took notes, so I didn't have to cram too much for exams the way some of my classmates had to. Overall, it had been a pretty halcyon four years.

I continued my building survey at Blair Hall, which housed the

English department, where I had taken many of my classes. The old Gothic building had undergone an unfortunate makeover in the 1960s, and a lot of the character you could see in old photographs had been stripped out—the wood moldings, the stone finials—and replaced with fluorescent lights and linoleum floors.

I documented the bathrooms there and finished as much of the survey as I could by before I had to hurry back to Friar Lake. Rochester jumped up and down in delight, and I took him out for a walk around the property and to check on Juan and Rigoberto. I found them relaxing in the cool of the chapel. "It's *muy caliente* out there, *jefe*," Rigoberto said. "We just take a break to cool down."

I didn't know what to say. They weren't my employees, and I wasn't familiar enough with their schedule. Instead of responding, I opted to remind them of the big meeting that afternoon. "Take one more look at the classroom and make sure it's clean," I said, and returned to my office.

Attendees for the meeting began arriving at three-fifteen. I left Rochester in my office and stood out in the parking lot directing faculty toward the classroom building and accepting their compliments about how beautiful the property was.

I recognized Oscar Panaccio from the design committee meeting, but I didn't think he knew I was his neighbor, and I was happy to keep it that way, when he grumbled, "Must cost a lot to keep a place like this up."

"We're actually a profit center for the college." I remembered Lili's admonition, and added some honey. "The money we bring in from renting the property out and running executive education programs helps pay the bills for your offices and classrooms."

He frowned and walked away. I knew his type, the kind of old guard professor who was against everything new, from online teaching to initiatives for special populations, like veterans and first-time-in-college students. The general complaint was that things had worked well at Eastern for over a century, so why change now?

Fortunately his was one of the lone dissenting voices about Friar Lake; most people had only nice things to say.

A few minutes before three-thirty I hurried to the classroom and stepped up to the podium. "Good afternoon," I said into the microphone, but the audience was too busy talking to each other to pay much attention.

I repeated the greeting, more forcefully, and that got more of the faculty to look up at me. I introduced myself, welcomed everyone to Friar Lake, and invited them to bring their professional association meetings there. Then I turned the session over to the committee chair.

I slipped out the back door to wait in the parking lot for any stragglers. Then I checked on Rochester through the window of my office – he was happily chewing on a rawhide bone. I went back to the classroom, where as Lili had predicted, an argument had broken out.

Oscar Panaccio was on his feet. He reminded me of the stereotype of professors when I was in college, in his brown sports jacket with leather elbow patches. I imagined that he smoked a pipe and drank sherry in the afternoons.

"I don't want anyone forcing me to write a recommendation for a student I don't respect or a program I don't think is worthwhile," he said.

"No one is going to require you to write a recommendation you don't want to," the chair said. She was a South Asian woman in a bright blue business suit. "But if you refuse, you'll have to provide a reason why. It can be student performance, or the quality of the program they're applying for. But you can't use personal bias as a reason."

"Who's going to say what personal bias is?" he demanded.

I backed out of the room as my phone buzzed with an incoming text. Rick wanted to know if I was free to meet him that evening at the Drunken Hessian. I figured I deserved a beer after my experience with the faculty senate, so I texted back that I could meet him at six-thirty.

The meeting was still going strong at five o'clock, and it wasn't until six that the chair called an end, apparently without having come to any kind of consensus. I stood by the door waiting for them all to leave so I could lock up. Oscar Panaccio and the Asian woman were still talking when everyone else had walked out. I was surprised at how much vitriol he was spewing, especially to a fellow professor and a woman of color.

His opinions were still stuck in the 1950s, about female students who dressed provocatively, frat brothers who shared papers with each other, and his opinion that race and economic background shouldn't affect college admissions. I guessed he was about seventy, and after I did the math I figured that meant he had gotten his PhD in the 1980s. He'd obviously missed the women's movement, the civil rights era, and the was pointedly ignoring all the social issues of the current times.

Maybe he'd been able to avoid all those because his academic discipline was biology, and the basics of what he taught hadn't changed. Or perhaps he was the kind of old fossil Eastern needed to get rid of in order to move forward.

I went up to the podium and shut down the computer and the projector, and they took the hint and walked outside. I shut down the lights, locked the door, and hurried past them back to my office to get Rochester.

They were still arguing when the dog and I walked to my car. There were two more vehicles in the lot, which I assumed belonged to them. Technically I should have waited for them to leave, but I was worried I'd be late to meet Rick, so I left them there.

As I did, though, I remembered the last meeting I had left that Oscar Panaccio had attended, and the man who had died afterward. I said a small prayer for the health of the faculty senate president.

15: First to Turn

I took Rochester out as soon as we got home, and then had some time to kill before going to meet Rick. Was there anyone else I need to research before I drove down to the Drunken Hessian? I looked at Rochester in the corner chewing on a bone and remembered the retainer he had found after the soccer team practice. That came from an orthodontist, right? And Todd Chatzky's widow was an orthodontist. Maybe my dog was trying to give me a clue.

I Googled Dr. Chatzky in Stewart's Crossing and got no results. But how could that be? Rick had specifically mentioned she was an orthodontist with an office on Main Street. I looked around my office for inspiration and spotted a photo of Lili and me. Of course. Todd's wife had kept her maiden name, at least for her practice.

I went back to Google and looked for orthodontist, Stewart's Crossing, and Dr. Wendilyn Jackson popped right up. I was a bit surprised that she was black, and just to be sure I Googled her name and "Chatzky" and came up with a couple of references.

One of them was a brand-new notice of a malpractice lawsuit filed against her. The parents of a young patient alleged that she had punctured his gum while fitting him for braces, and that she had overlooked the resulting infection until it required major surgery. I felt bad for her; it seemed like a reasonable consequence of so much poking and prodding at kids' mouths, but it had to be upsetting, especially coming at the same time as her husband's death.

By the time I finished that, I had to head down to the Drunken Hessian, where I found Rick already in a booth with a pair of Dogfish Head Amber Ale bottles. "I hope one of these is for me," I said. "You're looking pretty glum."

"Feeling that way, too," he said. "I hate murder investigations. I know last week I was grumbling about broken windows, but crime always hits me harder when there's a dead body involved."

He looked up at me and glared, and I held my hands up in front of me. "Hey, I'm not killing people. My dog just has a nose for finding bodies."

"Yeah, I'm sure that Jessica Fletcher had the same kind of excuse." Then he laughed. "You're not a crazed serial killer, are you? Because that would just be too much."

"Nope, I'm just an amateur sleuth." I picked up my bottle of beer and took a long drink. It was cold and refreshing.

"Speaking of which, come up with anything else I should look into?" he asked.

As usual, the server came over in the middle of our conversation. He was wearing the same pink shorts he had the last time we were in, but today's Hawaiian shirt was dark blue and featured dog breeds in a rotating pattern. I wanted it.

We ordered our cheeseburgers and when he was gone, I said, "I had an idea outside Hi Neighbor. What about Todd's wife? You said you were going to speak with her."

"Interesting situation," he said, between sips of beer. "At first she told me she was at home all evening, but then the security log showed she had showed up at River Bend at eight-thirty."

"After the meeting was over."

He nodded. "I asked her why she didn't tell the truth at first, and she said she was embarrassed because she and Todd argued, and she felt terrible that her last words to him were angry ones."

"Did she say what they were arguing about?"

"Just marriage stuff, she says."

"Nothing about her malpractice lawsuit?"

He put down his beer and wiped his hands on a napkin. "What did you find out?"

"She has a half-million-dollar suit against her." I explained about the kid with the gum infection. "But she probably has malpractice insurance to cover most of that."

He shook his head. "While I was waiting to speak with her I saw a sign in the lobby. A legal notice that she had chosen not to carry malpractice insurance, with a referral to the relevant statute."

"A judgment against her could destroy her practice," I said. "Did she say if Todd had life insurance?"

"Your mind works in very devious ways," he said. "I like that about you. I did ask her that, just as a matter of course. And yes, he had a million-dollar policy provided by his employer. With a double indemnity clause if he was killed at work."

"And he was killed at River Bend, his place of employment. I wonder if the double indemnity clause kicks in."

"Either way, it's enough to get her out of the hole with this lawsuit, and still have money left over."

The server delivered our burgers, and I sliced mine in half, doused it with ketchup, and took a big bite. "And there's no record of what time Dr. Jackson left River Bend, is there? She has motive and opportunity."

"That she does.

"As a dentist, she's accustomed to working with sharp instruments."

"Not necessarily a five-inch knife."

I nodded. "And that's not the kind of thing you'd carry in your purse."

"You never know what women have in there. Tamsen has everything from tissues and cough drops to one of those things that you use to break your car window if you get trapped inside. It has a wicked blade on it to cut the seatbelt, too, though the actual blade is shielded and can't be used as a weapon."

We talked about some of the other suspects in the case, including the bad-tempered Oscar Panaccio, and I told Rick about Panaccio's confrontation with the faculty senate president. As we finished, we wound our way back to Dr. Wendilyn Jackson. "For now, my money is on the widow," Rick said. "Especially now that I know about this malpractice case."

"And the double indemnity clause gives her a good reason to kill him at River Bend."

§ § § §

It rained again that night, and when I took Rochester out the next morning the grass was soaked, and on every block I noticed muddy ruts in the grass caused by the stand-up lawn mowers that the landscape service used.

It was just after sunrise, the air crisp with the tang of fall but still holding a bit of summer's warmth. We walked on the sunny side of the street as we headed up to the three lakes. I couldn't resist going back to where we'd discovered Todd Chatzky's body. By then the crime scene tape was gone and the walkway was open from one end to the other.

In the daylight, I noticed a drying puddle of machine oil that I'd missed the night before, where the sidewalk had a ramp down to street level. Tire tracks led forward a few feet along the sidewalk, until the oil under the tires wore out. Yet another example of the irresponsible way the landscapers ran amok around the community.

Rochester wanted to sniff over there but I had to pull him back because of the standing water in the grass between the sidewalk and the hedge that ran alongside. I didn't want his feet to get too wet, and who knew what kind of bacteria was growing there.

I wanted to get to Friar Lake early because that morning, we had guests arriving for a lunch sponsored by the Bucks County Association of Realtors. So of course I was frustrated getting out of River Bend, because the streets were like a slalom course. Before I could leave Sarajevo Court, I had to go around an appliance delivery, a roofer, and a mom in a minivan dropping her son off for a playdate. And each was parked on the opposite side of the street, so I had to zig and zag.

Rounding the corner I nearly ran smack into the back of a landscape vehicle, with long flatbed full of mowers behind it. River Bend had been built on reclaimed swampland, sandwiched between a nature preserve and an established suburban neighborhood, so land was at a premium, and our streets were very narrow – which didn't stop anyone from parking wherever they pleased.

When I first moved into the townhouse, security was quick to paper the windows of parking violators with yellow warning notices. They zoomed in on anyone who parked a few inches onto the grass or left a vehicle overnight in guest parking. Now, Friar Lake seemed as lawless as any third-world country, between the unregulated traffic, the shaggy landscaping—and the dead body Rochester and I had found.

I had to pass a humming vehicle advertising Mobile Monica's Place for Pampered Pets, a window installer, and a moving van before I made it out to the two well-defined lanes of River Bend Drive. Even that was jammed up with a tanker truck hosing down the sidewalk, a tree-trimmer in a bucket truck, and a PECO vehicle with electricians adjusting the incoming wires and a flagman who kept me waiting while a stream of incoming traffic passed.

The oaks, maples and willows along the River Road were still in brilliant shades of red and gold. The shorter sumacs were

Neil S. Plakcy

darker brown; I remembered an old childhood saying that the sumac was the first to turn color in the fall.

I saw Joey's truck parked back near his office and was relieved to see he was back. I let Rochester off the leash and we head back there. "How's your dad doing?" I asked as I walked in.

"He's going to rehab this afternoon, though he's resisting. Stubborn old coot thinks he can get better sitting around in his recliner at home. But that's not going to happen."

I thought of the Amy Winehouse song, about not wanting to go to rehab—though the kind of rehab she'd been singing about was different from what Joe Senior needed.

"They work you pretty hard in this rehab place, so the visiting hours are limited to late afternoon and evening. That means I'll be able to come back to work full-time tomorrow. How'd you do with the bathroom survey?"

"I'm almost finished, but my own work is piling up. I have a lot of requisitions to finish and I need to beat the bushes for more groups to rent this place out."

"I can finish the bathroom survey tomorrow. I've got my own paperwork to do here, but I want to be there to help them move my dad to the rehab facility and get him settled."

"How's Mark doing in all this?"

"He's holding the fort. Doing most of the Brody care – the food and the walks and the belly rubs. And my mom loves him, so she's been talking to him every day. She tells him things she doesn't want to tell me, like about the way her right hip hurts when she walks. She's going to need a hip replacement as soon as my dad gets better."

"Getting old isn't for sissies," I said.

On our way back to the office, Rochester made sure to walk through as much wet grass as he could find, which meant I had to dry his paws again before letting him loose in my office.

After clearing out some emails, I made sure that the caterer had access to the kitchen, and Joey, Rigoberto and Juan set up the tables and chairs in the chapel. The exterior of the property looked great, and sun streamed in through the newly-cleaned stained glass windows.

I stood there and surveyed my modest kingdom for a moment. For the first time in a while, I felt positive and relaxed about my job.

Then Rochester barked, and lay down on his side in the same position as we'd found Todd Chatzky's body, and I realized there was still a lot of work to be done.

16: All We Can Do

I missed most of the real estate speaker that morning because I was on the phone with my neighbor Epiphania about an upcoming program for the La Leche League. "What's the composition of your staff there?" she asked. "Male or female?"

"Does that matter? There are only four of us here full-time, all male."

"Just want to make sure no one is going to freak out if a bunch of our members pull out their boobs and start nursing during the program."

Personally, I was very boob-positive, and I figured Joey wouldn't mind. And Rigoberto and Juan didn't need to be in the building during the meeting. "I'll make a note for our caterer," I said. "Would you prefer all female servers?"

"That would be great, if you can manage it."

We went over a dozen more details. Epiphania was clearly a type-A personality. "Can I ask you what you did before you became a full-time mom?"

"I worked on Wall Street. I still do some freelance securities analysis, just to keep my hand in."

We finally finished our conversation and I slipped into the back of the chapel in time for the question and answer period. One woman stood up and said, "I have a lot of buyers who want new construction but don't want to be part of a homeowner's association. Are there any new properties coming up without one?"

"Why don't they want an HOA?" a man at a neighboring table asked. "HOAs maintain common area, keep up standards and mediate problems."

"Yes, but they also impose regulations and cause a lot of red tape. One of my buyers is a home breeder of bichon frises, and she doesn't want to be anywhere that a neighbor can complain about the number of dogs or the sound."

"Then she needs to be in one of those old farmhouses," the man said.

The woman looked frustrated. "My question still stands. Are there any new properties going up without HOAs?"

A discussion ensued, brokers and salespeople comparing notes. I could see the pluses and minuses of a homeowner's association—but right now at River Bend those were mostly minuses.

After the group left, I picked up the leftover business cards from the registration table and the caterer cleaned up. As I helped Joey, Rigoberto and Juan put away the folding tables and chairs, I noticed that Joey's eyes were heavy-lidded, and the corners of his mouth drooped. "What's the matter, bud?" I asked. "Something happen to your father?"

He shook his head. "For a guy who made such a fuss about going there, he turned into a big pussycat when the therapists started." He shook his head. "And after I warned them he was going to be a terror."

Rigoberto and Juan left us to clock out, and Joey and I began walking toward his office. "Then what?"

"How do you do it, Steve? You've been through a lot of crap in your life, and yet you usually have such a good attitude."

"So do you, Joey. You're probably the most cheerful, positive guy I know."

"But that's because nothing bad has ever happened to me. There's no reason to be unhappy when the world is sunny."

"Your dad is going to get better. You've always said he's a tough old bird."

"Yeah, but he's going to die eventually. And so is my mom. I know it's part of life, but I hate thinking about it. And that makes it hard to keep a positive attitude."

We reached his office and walked inside. "Come on, you must have had some problems in your past that you've overcome. What about coming out? That can't have been easy for you." I sat down across from him.

"Compared to other guys, like Mark, it was a breeze." Joey sat back in his chair. "I started figuring out that I was interested in guys rather than girls when I was about fourteen or fifteen. I was a big jock, mostly baseball, and I started getting these weird feelings in the locker room, seeing other guys naked."

He blew out a breath. "I decided I wanted to see if I was really gay, so I looked around and picked out this one kid, Eddie Safran, who everybody teased because he was kind of girly and wore goth eye makeup. He was in my math class, and I went up to him after class one day and told him that I wanted to be his friend, and that if anybody picked on him he should tell me, and I'd take care of it."

"That was sweet of you."

"I had an ulterior motive, of course. I invited Eddie over to my house one afternoon to help me with math homework and in the middle of a problem I leaned over and kissed him."

He looked at me as if he was worried I was going to freak out, but I said, "I'm assuming a wild make out session ensued."

"Yeah. I mean, I liked him, once I got to know him. He had a wicked sense of humor. We used to watch gay porn videos together and then practice on each other. So I never had much angst about being gay, though I didn't tell anybody what I was doing with Eddie, and he didn't either. We were just math buddies to everybody at school."

"And Eddie was okay with that, I assume?"

"Oh yeah. His parents were immigrants and they were very narrow-minded. He was smart, and when we graduated he got into Duke, and I got into Penn State. That year was an Olympic summer, and I was watching the swimming and diving with my dad. I was really getting into seeing the guys in their Speedos, and when this Australian diver, Matthew Mitcham, won a gold medal they announced that he was the first openly gay Olympic champion."

"I remember that. It was a big deal."

Joey nodded. "So I said that was cool, that gay guys could be great athletes, too, and my dad agreed with me. And then I said, so that means I can be gay and still play baseball at Penn State."

"Well, that's one way to come out to your dad. What did he say?"

"He said that I could fuck zebras if I wanted, and I'd still be his son."

I burst out laughing. "Not exactly the same thing."

"Not unless you're talking about referees," Joey said. "So that was that. By the time I got to Penn State I was out, and I made the roster my freshman year, but I didn't get to play much and I didn't bother to try out as a sophomore because I had other stuff I was more interested in."

"So you've really never had anything bad happen to you?"

He shook his head. "I mean, my grandparents all died, and an aunt I liked, and I was sad, but none of those things rocked my world like this." He looked at me. "So what's the secret, Steve? How do you keep a positive attitude when you run into something that makes you really miserable?"

"I can't give you a lot of advice," I said. "After Mary's second miscarriage, I was as bitter as a sliced radish. Angry at the world, angry at her, even though it wasn't her fault. Then I went to prison, and that pretty much wiped me out."

He shook his head. "I can't even imagine what that must have been like."

"It was grim. But I saw all these guys who were in worse shape than I was. Guys with life sentences, with no education, with nobody on the outside who cared about them. I had my dad, and one friend from business school, and I realized I only had to get through the rest of my term and I could start over."

Remembering those days gave me a hollow feeling in the pit of my stomach, but I soldiered on. "And then I came back to Stewart's Crossing, and I was still miserable. But a professor of mine at Eastern remembered me and gave me a part-time job as an adjunct, and then Rochester came into my life, and then Lili."

I smiled. "You've got a big head start on happiness. You still have both your parents, and they love you. So does Mark, and so does Brody. You have an education, you have skills. And outside of today, you have a positive attitude about life. Add all those together and you can face anything."

"Even losing my dad?"

"Even that. To be honest, even losing Mark."

He shuddered. "Don't want to think about that."

"In a way, it's like taking a dog into your life," I said. "Sometimes I look at Rochester and I realize he's already five or six years old, and big dogs like him don't have the longest life spans. I think how awful it would be to lose him, and it will be—it's going to be horrible, I know that. So I try and love him as much as I can while I have him."

I remembered Todd Chatzky, and how quickly and unexpectedly his life had been wiped out. "We have to think that about everyone around us."

"I can try to do that," Joey said.

Neil S. Plakcy

"That's all any of us can do."

17: Being Present

When I went back to my office, I settled into my chair and looked out the big glass window at Friar Lake. From the gatehouse I could see all the way through the property, down the paved paths, past the Gothic-style chapel, to the dormitories where the monks had lived.

Had those monks been happy, I wondered? Were there complaints against the abbot, the cellarer, a brother who snored through evening prayers? Or had they managed to live simple lives without argument, working together for the common good?

Back then, I assumed, if they had disputes, they were addressed in person, rather than through an electronic intermediary. Was that better, or worse?

I was in my office for about an hour when Joey showed up. "When things go wrong between you and Lili, how do you handle them?" he asked, as he sunk into the chair across from me. Rochester got up and rested his head on Joey's knee.

"What's the problem?"

"It seems like we argue about everything lately. Whose turn is it to take the laundry to the laundromat? I let Mark sleep late, so why can't he make the bed when he gets up? Do we really want to buy a house together when every little thing sets us off?"

I blew out a breath. "Those are both large and small questions. I try to start with that saying about don't sweat the small stuff. But I know that's not terribly helpful."

Joey frowned. "It's not."

"But you can handle the small stuff pretty easily. Put up a calendar on your fridge and mark things off when you do them."

"That's so petty, though."

"I understand. But sometimes it's the petty stuff that makes you crazy, and if you can keep track of it, that's one less irritation." I smiled. "Unless, of course, you forget to mark things off on the calendar."

"Not helping."

"The real solution is to talk about what's bothering you," I said. "What is it?"

"I don't know," Joey said, with agony in his voice. "I know I've been stressed with my father in the hospital, but he's my dad, and even when my brothers volunteer to help I want to be there. Mark says it's a control issue and that I have to learn to let go."

I thought for a minute. "Sometimes when I get caught up in something, I'm not really present with Lili when I should be. I mean, we'll be at dinner together, and I'll be in my head thinking about a question, and she'll start to get irritated."

That had happened more times than I wanted to admit, especially when, as we were then, Rochester and I were nose to the ground on the trail of a criminal. "Does that sound like something that's going on with you and Mark?"

He sighed. "Maybe. I know I've been trying not to burden him with things that I'm worrying about."

"The problem is when you're worrying about something and the other person doesn't know what it is, the other person can think it's them."

I shook my head. "That grammar was terrible. If you're upset about your dad, you should share those feelings with Mark. That's what a relationship is all about. And if you tell him you're stressed about your dad, he won't worry that it's something he said or did that's bothering you."

"I hate this stuff about sharing feelings," Joey said. "In the past it hasn't been a problem for me, because, well, I have a pretty happy-go-lucky attitude toward the world, and Mark is the one who worries about everything."

"It's new territory for you, but that doesn't mean you can't grow a pair and man up," I said. "Talk to him. You're going to buy a house together. You need to be on the same page whenever possible."

He stood up, shaking out his big frame. "I'll give it a try."

My first year at Eastern, I lived in an all-male dorm called Birthday House, full of young guys on their own for the first time, full of testosterone and unaccustomed freedom. No parents to dictate bedtimes or homework, only a couple of resident advisors who were barely older than we were, and unable to control us. I'd gotten into trouble a couple of times, culminating in a wild naked run around the exercise track with a bunch of my buddies after a few too many beers.

That hadn't ended well, and I learned a couple of lessons that helped the next time I was pushed into an all-male environment, courtesy of the California state penal system. Keep my head down and my mouth shut. Look for allies who would keep me out of trouble. Avoid conflict at all costs.

In a sense, that was what I was advising Joey, too. I assumed that was how the monks worked things out, too. When I got home, I practiced what I had preached to Joey. I put all my worries aside, about Friar Lake and River Bend, and focused on being present for Lili.

She noticed the difference at dinner. "You've been so preoccupied lately but it feels like you're more here than usual. Is that my imagination?"

I told her about my conversation with Joey, and she nodded approvingly. "You should have more talks like that."

"With you?"

"If you like."

And so we sprawled on the sofa, and talked about the photography exhibition she'd gone to in New Hope the week before, and how it might influence her own work. We talked about a mystery novel I was reading when I had the chance, and about Rochester's behavior on walks.

The ordinary stuff of daily life, but it was very relaxing. Those good feelings carried over into my work on Thursday, and I was able to get through a lot of paperwork and emails without feeling stressed.

That evening after dinner, Rick called and asked if he could come over. "Only if you bring Rascal," I said. "Rochester needs some play time."

"Good to know where I stand with you. Be there in a half hour."

As usual, Rochester alerted to Rick's arrival long before I heard his truck pull into the driveway. He started barking like mad, and the only thing that shut him up was when I opened the front door and Rascal rushed in. The two of them took off on a mad dash up the staircase, toenails clicking on the wood.

Lili kissed Rick's cheek and said she was going to head upstairs. I offered Rick a beer from the fridge and took one for myself, and we sat in the living room. "What's up?" I asked.

"Mostly I just need to vent, and Tamsen's off at a trade show in Vegas."

He sipped his beer. "This morning I was out doing surveillance at a bus stop near Crossing Commons. We had a report some of the kids had been getting into trouble while waiting for the bus."

Crossing Commons was the first apartment complexes in Stewart's Crossing, and had been around since I was a teenager. Back then, it attracted what people called "the lower classes," which meant somebody who couldn't afford to buy a house. Though it had been completely renovated a few years before, the rumor was that some of the tenants were there on Section 8 vouchers, which made people suspicious.

"You find anything?"

"Yeah. Caught a couple of boys trying to knock down a stop sign by swinging their backpacks at it."

"Did you arrest them?"

He shook his head. "They hadn't managed to do any damage. But I gave them both a serious talking to. One of them plays football and I put the fear of his coach in his head. Hopefully it'll work."

The dogs came scrambling back down the stairs and chased each other around the dining room table a couple of times. We watched them for a couple of minutes, until they suddenly collapsed together in a pile in the middle of the living room.

"Any news about Todd Chatzky's murder?" I asked Rick, when the dogs were settled.

"Nothing. One minute I'm convinced it's the widow. She has means, motive and opportunity, but at the same time, she's genuinely broken up about her husband's death." He sipped his beer again. "Then I think about all the stuff going on here at River Bend, and I have a gut feeling that all the problems you've pointed out must have some connection."

"I still have some more data to review. Want to look it over with me?"

"Why not? I'll get to see your computer wizardry at work."

"Hardly wizardry," I said. "Just boring data analysis."

We moved over to the dining room table, where I turned on my laptop and brought up the material I had downloaded from the Hi Neighbor website.

Rick and I read together in silence, until he said, "There are a lot of complaints about renters, aren't there?" he asked. "Your neighbors don't seem to like them."

"There's a general problem with renters," I said. "Not that I'm stereotyping, but in general, because they don't have an investment in the property, they don't care as much about stuff like taking care of things the association doesn't handle, like planting flowers. And often they're younger than the average home-owner, so they play music too loud."

Rick pointed to the screen. "This one complains about a dog left outside who barks all day. And there's a whole bunch who are mad that people don't put their trash cans out at the right time or on the right day."

"You see how narrow these streets are," I said. "They're just wide enough that two cars can pass each other comfortably. When people leave their trash cans out in the street, or pile up debris that spills out, it can make the streets like slalom courses."

We read together. Sometimes, the complainant was clear. "I live at 1515 Bucharest Place and renters moved into the townhouse next door to me six months ago. They leave their small child in the courtyard and the baby cries with a piercing shriek. I've complained to the management office and they tell me to call the landlord, but the only name they have is a corporation with a post office box and no phone number."

In others, it wasn't. "One of renters on my street has a teenage boy who bounces a ball on his garage every night at midnight for at least an hour. Security says it's his property so he can do what he wants."

I pointed to the name at the end of the complaint. "Hi Neighbor requires you to log in with your real name, rather than an online handle, and they validate with some database somewhere to make sure you either live here or own property here."

I opened a new browser and plugged in the name of the woman who complained about the teenage boy. "This woman, Arlene Locano, lives on Prague Place. That's the first street in from Ferry Road."

Rascal got up from the floor and nosed his dad, which caused

Rochester to do the same thing with me.

"Fascinating as this is, I'll leave the analysis to you," Rick said. "If anyone new jumps out at you with a motive to kill Mr. Chatzky, you'll let me know."

"I will indeed."

I let Rick and Rascal out, and sat on the floor with Rochester, scratching behind his ears. "You had a good time with your friend," I said.

He looked up at me with his big brown eyes. I remembered a cartoon I had seen online, two dogs talking to each other. The first one say, "What if I die before I find out who's a good boy?"

Since then, I'd changed my comments to Rochester. Instead of phrasing them as questions, I made statements. "You're a good boy. Daddy loves you."

I maintained to anyone who'd listen that my dog really understood me, so it seemed a reasonable adjustment.

18: Low Ball Offer

Friday afternoon when I had some free time, I returned to the Hi Neighbor information I had been looking at with Rick the night before. Since he'd pointed out so many of the comments were about renters, I created a new spreadsheet and began making notes of homes that were being rented. It was anecdotal information at first—neighbors complaining about neighbors. Eventually I knew I'd have to go into the Bucks County Property Appraiser and see who owned those properties. And maybe I could get a full list of renters from Todd's secretary Lois, or ask Rick to get it.

The sun began dipping down outside my window, spreading a golden glow on the grassy lawns and shedding trees. Rochester sat up once and barked as Rigoberto and Juan left in their rundown sedan.

Then he found one of his peanut-butter bones, settled down on the floor in front of my desk, and began chewing loudly. I did one last check of college emails, then closed my spreadsheet and called Joey. We agreed we could shut the property down for the weekend. On my way home, I stopped at the IGA grocery in the center of Stewart's Crossing to pick up a bouquet of yellow and orange chrysanthemums for Lili—because I wanted to.

She was happily surprised by the gesture, and we went out to dinner at a chain steakhouse out on the highway. "What's new in the wonderful world of Steve?" Lili asked as we ate our salads.

"I've been going through all the posts on Hi Neighbor," I said. "I never realized there were so many problems, or so many people with complaints. It's like reading Dear Abby, only without the resolutions."

"And all those complaints still don't motivate you to do something? Like run for the board?"

"I'm doing what I can," I said. "Putting together this information for Rick. Trying to see if anyone who posted had a motive to kill Todd Chatzky."

"Do you think things will improve at River Bend with him gone?"

The server appeared to take away our salad plates, which gave me a minute to think. "I don't know. First I have to figure out if Todd was the source of the problems, or if it was the board."

"I think the whole system is screwed up," Lili said. "When people complained to Todd, he put the blame on the board. But when people went to the association meetings, the board pushed the blame back on Todd and Pennsylvania Properties."

"There has to be an answer somewhere," I said. "If I keep tugging on threads I believe a pattern is going to show up."

Lili raised her water glass to me. "Good luck with that."

§§§§

Saturday morning, Rochester let me sleep in until eight o'clock, and we walked up toward the twin lakes in crisp autumn sunshine. As we got close, we ran into Drew Greenbaum and his mother's corgi Lilibet. While the dogs played I asked how his mom was doing.

"No better," he said. "She's in a rehab place for her broken hip, but I really need to get her into a senior living place with a memory care wing. Which I can't do until I sell her house."

"Any luck getting the liens removed?"

"I talked to the board president, that guy in the wheelchair."

"Earl Garner."

"Yeah, that's the guy. He said he could make me a deal if I'd sell the house to him. He'd 'take care' of the liens." Drew wiggled his index fingers to represent the verbal quotes.

"Pay them off?"

"Or something. He's the president of the board. Who knows what he can do?"

"You going to take the offer?"

"Not sure yet. I'm meeting with a Realtor this morning to discuss my options." I wondered if it would be one of the ones who'd been at Friar Lake for the lunch, and how that person felt about HOAs.

For my part, I had been happy with the way the community had been run for most of the time I'd lived there. I didn't start paying attention until things began to go wrong, and I wondered if that was the way many of my neighbors had been, too.

When we got back to the house, Lili was on her way out. "Heading to New York to get my hair cut at that place Andrea del Presto recommended." She leaned up and kissed my cheek. "I'll grab something for breakfast at the train station in Trenton. See you later."

She was gone in a whirlwind of Chanel's Chance perfume, the scent lingering in the air for a few minutes. I fixed Rochester his chow, had a muffin, and then turned back to my computer.

I finished assembling the spreadsheet of rental addresses, and then turned to the property appraiser's website. The first address I checked, the home of the screaming baby, got me no further—it was owned by 1517 Bucharest Place, LLC. Well, that was irritating. I'd have to go to the Pennsylvania Department of State to research the ownership of the LLC.

The next address was easier – it was owned by Oscar Panaccio.

Before I went any further, I searched for his name, just to make sure I hadn't put in his home address by accident, and discovered that he owned five properties in River Bend, all townhouses.

Two of them matched complaints I'd found on Hi Neighbor. Interesting, that he was on a committee that dispatched fines while at the same time he was a landlord who generated complaints. There wasn't a committee for general complaints like noise violations; those went directly to the property manager.

I went back to my search and quickly discovered a pattern. Twelve houses in River Bend, from single-family homes to townhouses, were owned by limited liability companies named after the property address, including one on Sarajevo Court a few doors down from mine.

When I moved in, the people who lived there were an elderly couple, the Camerons. Mr. Cameron had a bichon frise who he walked all around the community, and he waved at every car he passed. He was a regular fixture of River Bend, and I was surprised one day when I saw a younger man come out of the Camerons' townhouse with the dog on a leash.

Neighborhood scuttlebutt—pre Hi Neighbor–provided the details. Mr. Cameron had suffered a stroke, and his stepson had moved in to help while he recovered. When Mr. Cameron came home from the hospital he'd lost at least fifty pounds and needed a walker.

The stepson, a chain smoker, walked the dog morning and night. Then one day an ambulance appeared at the Cameron house and the news wasn't good. Mr. Cameron suffered a stroke and died.

Things went downhill quickly from there. Within months, the stepson was diagnosed with lung cancer—once again taken away in an ambulance, according to a neighbor. We learned that his cancer was at an advanced stage, and he never returned.

Mrs. Cameron hired a dog walker, and neighbors pitched in to take her to church and grocery shopping. But her age and poor health caught up with her, and she was dead within a year after her husband. I realized I'd never seen a For Sale sign on the house and had assumed it had gone to some distant relative.

I switched over to the state's corporation database and found nothing of use. In each case, the sole owner of the LLC was another corporation, this one headquartered in Delaware. Corporate regulations there were notoriously lax, probably because legend had it that DuPont had controlled the state for decades.

I was stymied. I couldn't learn anything useful about the LLCs from either Pennsylvania or Delaware. There had to be a way I could learn something, though. I knew that new buyers had to be approved by the HOA, so surely somewhere in their records there was a connection between the LLC and the human being behind it.

When I first came to live at River Bend and transferred the deed to the townhouse into my own name, I went into the office for an interview. I had filled out a form, and one of my new neighbors, from the approvals committee, had met with me and filled out a form herself. Were those forms online?

My fingertips tingled. I was pretty sure I could hack into the HOA website; I'd visited it a few times to look for information and had noted that the security wasn't very good. The only time the https prefix came up, the one that indicated you were on a secure website, was when you switched over to the Pennsylvania Properties site to make payments.

Or I could just ask Lois if she had a list, and if she'd share it with me.

I looked at the clock. It was almost eleven, and I knew that the HOA office was open until noon on Saturday. I gave Rochester a green dental stick to chew and hopped into my car. The sun was high in a nearly cloudless sky, and a light breeze ruffled the remaining red and gold leaves of the maples and oaks along River Bend Drive.

There was a party out by the pool, and the few parking spaces not taken up by landscaping vehicles were all full. I parked by the curb and hurried inside. Lois wasn't at her desk, and I was surprised to see Earl Garner in Todd's office. "I'm busy here, and Lois has the day off," Garner said brusquely. "You'll have to come back on Monday for whatever you need."

And good morning to you, too, I thought. I held up my hand. "No problem."

Yeah. No problem for me. I'd get that list of names the way I wanted.

19: Neatsfoot Oil

Lili was still at the hairdresser in New York, so I could retrieve my hacker laptop, do what I needed, and have it put away before she came home. At least that's the way I justified it.

I set the ladder up in the hallway outside the second bathroom and climbed up, pushing away the hatch that led to the attic crawl space, where I kept it stowed away, so that I'd have to make a conscious effort to retrieve it.

Rochester slumped behind me in the second floor hallway, as if he knew I was up to something and needed to be watched carefully.

The laptop wasn't quite so secret as it had been – Rick and Lili both knew that it existed. It had once belonged to Caroline Kelly, Rochester's first mom, and after she died I loaded my hacking tools on it and used what I learned online to help Rick figure out who killed her. I kept it in the attic so that I would have to make a conscious choice to retrieve it and use the tools on it, and so that I'd have to think twice about retrieving it.

Since then I had used the tools there occasionally, for the most part in legal pursuits. I justified my exploit because I was a homeowner at River Bend, and I ought to have access to this information on that basis. And if there was a connection to Todd's murder, I had a moral obligation to pursue it.

That explanation wouldn't have held up in a court of law if Rick needed to use the information, and if I was caught I'd have to hire a very savvy attorney. But I was confident that the tools I had could hide my identity and my IP address enough so that no one would notice I'd dipped in and retrieved the information I needed. Lili was in New York, and while I wouldn't lie to her if the question came up, I didn't have to justify myself to her the way I might if she was there.

Act first, apologize later. And if I found something useful for Rick, I'd wiggle around until I found a legal way to deliver the information to him.

While I waited for the old laptop to turn on, I considered what I had to do. First, I had to set up a VPN, a virtual private network, that would protect me while I was online. The one I used, a commercially available one for which I paid a monthly fee of a couple of dollars, promised that their strict zero-logs policy would keep my identity under wraps while I was online. Primarily it was designed to protect your online data while banking, paying credit card bills and so on, but it meant that no one could track my activity online back to me and my home's IP address.

Once the VPN was running, I set up a port scanner and aimed it at the River Bend HOA website. Essentially, a port is like a doorway into your home, and a port scanner knocks on every port on a network to see if it's available for entry. The port scanner can also reveal the presence of security devices like firewalls that stand between the sender and the target. This technique is known as fingerprinting.

There was a firewall around the HOA site, but it was a cheap commercial one that came with the purchase of a bunch of computer tools, and whoever installed it either hadn't followed the instructions, or hadn't been keeping up with regular updates, because I had my choice of three different ports that would let me in.

I could have found out information like the operating system the computer was using, the internet service provider the HOA used, and how long that particular computer had been online. But all I cared about was getting a look at the root directory – what on a regular computer would be considered the C: drive.

When your browser sends a message to a website, it generally displays an HTML page which contains directions on what to show you—what images, what text, what other features like video content. That page sits in the root directory of the hard drive where the website is housed. I wanted to see what else was in that root directory—for example, folders of information about homeowners.

Rochester kept nuzzling me, and it was hard to work one handed, while the other scratched behind his ears. I had to nudge him aside with my knee and focus on typing in the right commands.

At some point, after all the current fuss blew over, I'd have to volunteer to help the association with the community's website and install some better security, without revealing how I knew it was necessary. For the moment, I let my fingers dance over the keyboard, searching for the files I was interested in.

I downloaded a spreadsheet of renters and one of owners. But I was worried that they'd only have the name of the LLCs who owned the property, not the person, or persons, behind them. So I kept snooping.

It was almost too easy to find a folder called "Interviews," where all the forms filled out by the new owners and the board members had been scanned and uploaded. I quickly downloaded the folder and shut down the laptop, not wanting to stay connected to the HOA site for a minute longer than necessary. I had learned through years of experience that the longer you remained somewhere you didn't belong, the greater the chance that you could be discovered.

If, for example, one of the board members was logged in legitimately to the site, he or she could easily see who else was online at the time. If that person was savvy enough to recognize that my VPN address wasn't on the list of authorized users, my hack could be discovered. I might not be implicated directly, but it would be a way for that person, or the board, to note that someone was looking into protected information.

I took the laptop back up to the attic and returned the ladder to the garage. Rochester followed me the whole time. "There. You satisfied?" I asked him.

He didn't say anything, just looked up at me with those big brown eyes of his. I leaned down and petted him. "I know you're watching out for me, puppy. And I appreciate it. But sometimes I've got to do what I've got to do."

There were over seven hundred homes and townhouses in River Bend, and the folder of interview sheets contained nearly two thousand forms. How could I ever get through all of those on my own? It would take hours, maybe days.

I looked over to where Rochester was nosing under the sofa, searching for a bone he'd accidentally kicked under there. I got up, moved the sofa, and he pounced on the bone, which looked pretty much like every other bone on the living room floor. "See, your search paid off," I said.

I smiled at him, and he began to chew. Search, I realized. That's what I needed to do. I could do a basic search from my own computer, without any special tools. I set up the computer to look through the PDF files for the word LLC, and then sat back, very pleased with myself.

While I waited, I thought about what else I could do. Oscar Panaccio owned a couple of properties in River Bend; perhaps that meant he knew who else did. How could I reach out to him?

I looked over at Rochester, who was chewing happily, while surrounded by bones and toys. But I knew that if I gave him a new one, he'd jump right on that.

Maybe Oscar would, too. Suppose I emailed him, mentioned that I knew him through Eastern, and that I was considering selling my townhouse. I could invite him over on that pretense, and then sound him out.

I logged into my Eastern College email. It wasn't the most effective way to get a response from him, but it was logical. I sent him the message, and then sat on the floor to play with Rochester.

We were playing tug-a-rope when Lili got home from New York. Her hair, usually so exuberant, was flat and wet, and so were her Italian leather jacket and her skinny jeans. She looked drenched, even though the sun was shining outside. "What happened?" I asked, as I jumped up to take the leather jacket from her.

"I had to park in a far lot at the Trenton train station, and when I was halfway to my car it just started to pour." She caught a glimpse of herself in the sliding glass door and started to cry. "I look terrible!"

"It's not that bad," I said, as she ran for the stairs.

I stood there holding her dripping jacket. One of the things I loved about Lili was that though she had a fiery personality, she almost never cried. My ex-wife had been a crier, and I always felt so helpless when she burst into tears, whether they were because of something I'd said, her hormones, or the general feeling of loss that pervaded our marriage in its later years.

I could deal with the jacket, though. I found a padded hanger in the downstairs closet and hung the jacket up in the half bathroom off the dining room. I began to blot off the excess moisture, and while I did I had an inspiration. I found my phone and called Tamsen. She was such a kind person, and always looked so perfectly put together that I was sure she'd be able to help Lili salvage her fancy cut.

"A bit of an emergency," I said, and explained what had happened. "You think you could come over and give Lili some sisterly advice?"

"I'm at Justin's Pop Warner game, but I can duck out for this. Be there in a few."

Neil S. Plakcy

Rochester knew something was wrong, and he kept threading his way around my feet. I went back to the bathroom and continued drying Lili's jacket, and he slumped on the tile beside me.

The jacket was one of her prized possessions; she'd told me how during her first marriage, when she was living in Milan, she had stumbled on a designer's private sale and talked her way in. She had spotted the jacket and fallen in love with it, and even though she was nearly broke and the jacket wiped out her bank account, she bought it.

Tamsen arrived as I was finishing the blotting effort. I sent her upstairs and heard her knock on the bedroom door. "Lili? It's Tamsen. Can I come in?"

I didn't hear the response, but the door opened and closed so I assumed it had been a positive one. Then I retrieved a tub of neatsfoot oil from the garage. I had a boss once in California who had sung its praises, though he had a heavy Southern accent and pronounced the last word "awl." Since then I'd found it came in handy for treating any kind of leather.

Rochester did not like the scent, and he left me and went upstairs, where I heard him plop on the floor—I assumed in front of the bedroom door. I heard the dim whirr of a blow dryer and hoped Tamsen was working her magic on Lili's new do.

By the time I had massaged the oil deeply into the leather, the door opened upstairs. "Thank you so much, Tamsen," Lili said. "I feel a whole lot better."

"And you look terrific, too. That's a very flattering cut for you."

They came down the stairs, Rochester threading his way between them. "Wow," I said when I saw Lili. Her hair was much straighter than usual, though still with a gentle wave, and the stylist had cut it into a bob that made her look like a 1920s flapper. "That's an amazing cut."

"I'm sure I couldn't style it as well as the guy in New York did, but it does look good, doesn't it?" Tamsen asked.

I kissed her cheek. "Thanks for saving the day."

She looked at her watch. "The game's about to finish. I need to hustle to pick up the guys."

After she left, Lili turned to me. "You really like it?"

"Honey, you know I think you're the most beautiful woman in the world, and I'm incredibly lucky you put up with me and Rochester. I love your hair in curls—but this new look is pretty awesome, too."

"Thanks for calling Tamsen," she said. "I was so upset—I felt like I'd wasted all that time and money." She sniffed the air. "What's that smell?"

"Neatsfoot oil. I dried your jacket and I'm moisturizing the leather now."

"You really are a lifesaver, aren't you?" She took my hand. "Why don't you come upstairs with me and let me show you how much I appreciate you." She smiled. "Just be careful with the hair."

20: *Property Values*

I didn't get a chance to check on the search results from the PDF files until after dinner. My laptop had gone into sleep mode, and when I woke it I discovered it had found thirty-five examples of LLC in the scanned interview forms. Eager as I was to look through them, Lili was upstairs, and I figured that she still needed some reassurance, so I spent the time with her instead.

Sunday morning Lili reminded me we had promised to join Mark and Joey on a trip to a big flea market in Bryn Mawr, in a neighborhood of Philadelphia that took its name from a railroad called the Main Line. The name had become a metonym for the series of wealthy towns it passed through. When you said Main Line, you meant more than just the railroad; the term conjured up images of wealth and privilege. One of my favorite movies, *High Society*, with Grace Kelly, Bing Crosby and Louis Armstrong, was set there.

"Tell me again why we're going all the way to Bryn Mawr?" I grumbled to Lili over breakfast. "Lambertville is a lot closer."

Throughout my childhood my mom, dad and I spent Sunday afternoons at the flea market in Lambertville, upriver from Stewart's Crossing, though on the Jersey side of the Delaware. My mother collected Lenox china, Lalique crystal, and a host of other knickknacks. I looked through boxes of books, often paperbacks with the covers ripped off that retailed for a dime or a quarter.

My father always had an eye out for tools. He'd walk up to

a table full of wrenches, screwdrivers, pliers and other ordinary stuff, and pick out the strange one in the bunch. He'd hold it up and ask the guy behind the table, "What does this do?"

Usually the owner would say something like, "Damned if I know."

"How much do you want for it?" my dad would ask. If the price was right, he'd buy it and add it to his collection. Any time something broke around the house, or I needed my bike adjusted or a toy fixed, my dad had the tool and the skill to handle the repair.

When he sold the townhouse, he sold off most of his tools, too. I wondered if he had ever found out what those oddball tools did, or simply passed them on to some other curious soul.

"This Bryn Mawr market is a once a year thing," Lili said. "A big benefit for a local charity. According to Mark, the rich people all donate stuff and he can pick up a lot of merchandise for his store."

"Are we taking the dogs?"

"Joey says yes," Lili said. "Apparently the property is spread out enough that as long as we keep them on a close leash they can go with us. And this is a compromise with Joey—that he's taking a day off from obsessing about his dad to do something fun."

I leaned down to scratch behind Rochester's ears. "You want to see your buddy Brody?" I asked, and he opened his mouth in a broad doggy grin. "Well, that's it. Rochester wants to see Brody, so I guess we're going."

Mark picked us up a half hour later in the van he used to transport merchandise. As soon as he opened the back door, Brody jumped out and began to chase Rochester around the driveway. "Come back here, Bro," Joey said.

Brody ignored him. He was having too much fun. "Rochester, come here." I knelt and sent him some kissing noises. He looked up at me and started back, but then Brody woofed, and Rochester was distracted.

"Your dog is a troublemaker," I said to Mark. I was worried because Brody and Rochester were roaming farther down the street. I trusted Rochester, but I was worried that he'd get too caught up in chasing Brody and get himself in trouble.

"Brody, come!" Mark said in that authoritative voice, and Brody immediately turned and high-tailed it right to Mark, who grabbed his collar. "Good boy." He leaned down and kissed the top of Brody's pure-white head.

Rochester was right behind him, and we loaded them both into the back of the van. Mark had rigged up a mesh net that created a separate area for the dogs, but while the van was empty, they had the run of the back. "We have a good cop, bad cop thing going on with Brody," Joey apologized. "You can guess which one I am."

"You just have to be stricter with him," Mark said. "You give in too easily. To everybody."

"Look, I'm here, aren't I?" Joey asked. "I'm not at the hospital. I'm not over at the high school playing pickup basketball."

"If you'd rather be at either of those places," Mark began.

"Don't start," Joey interrupted him. "Just drive."

I shared a glance with Lili as we climbed into the van—Mark and Joey up front, Lili and me in the seats behind them. I hoped they weren't going to argue all day.

The dogs romped around the back together for a few minutes, then settled down by the time we were on the highway. "Do you know there's a mnemonic for the towns of the Main Line?" Mark asked as he drove. I wondered if he was consciously trying to shift the conversation away from his problems with Joey.

"You mean like Every Good Boy Does Fine for the lines of the treble clef?" I asked. "My piano teacher would be so proud I remember that, even if I can't play a note anymore."

"Exactly. The mnemonic for the stations of the Main Line is

Old Maids Never Wed And Have Babies, Period."

"Excuse me?" Lili said, laughing. "Not exactly politically correct, is it?"

"It's old-fashioned," Mark said. "Overbrook, Merion, Narberth, Wynnewood, Ardmore, Haverford, Bryn Mawr, Paoli. Hopefully, lots of rich people from all along the Main Line will have donated merchandise to this fair. This year's beneficiary is a group called Alpha Bravo Canines, which trains service dogs and donates them to disabled veterans."

"You'll have to spend a lot of money then," I said. "Sounds like a great charity."

"Only if I can find bargains," Mark said.

"Don't worry, he'll find something to spend money on," Joey grumbled, but there didn't seem to be much rancor in his tone.

It was one of the last gorgeous days of Indian summer, sunny but cool and crisp. We arrived at the market and parked at the end of a long line of cars. There was plenty of room between the tables, most of them managed by individuals and families cleaning out their attics. A couple of churches and a synagogue had tables, too, as well as a few neighborhood groups.

Mark had brought a sheaf of cash with him, and he dispensed it liberally. Periodically Joey and I were delegated to carry pieces of furniture back to the van as well as tote bags full of smaller items.

"Just call us the Sherpas," Joey said, as we hefted the sides of a round mahogany table with claw feet.

"I get to be Tenzing Norgay," I said. "I always thought he didn't get enough credit for climbing Everest with Edmund Hillary."

"That's fine. I don't even know the names of any other Sherpas."

We walked with the table between us, excusing ourselves and dodging around elderly couples and young women with tiny dogs on long leashes.

"You and Mark getting along all right?" I asked, when we reached the truck.

He shrugged. "We're both under a lot of stress because of my dad's being sick. I'm over at the hospital or the rehab all the time, and Mark has been complaining about Brody. He is a handful, I'll admit."

"Couples go through things like that all the time," I said. "As long as you keep communicating with Mark, you'll be fine. And any time you have the urge to argue, count to ten and really look at him. Look for whatever caused you to fall in love with him. I guarantee by the time you get to ten you won't be so angry anymore."

"Are the Sherpas Buddhist?" he asked. "Because that sounds like very Buddhist advice."

"I'm pretty sure they're Tibetan Buddhists," I said. "And I think you'd have to be pretty philosophical to live in such an unforgiving climate."

That afternoon, Lili bought a big coffee table book of Ansel Adams photos, and I found one of the small Lenox birds my mother had collected, though in a color and a pose I didn't have. I was sure she was smiling down from heaven that I was adding to her collection.

Lili and I had a great time at the flea market, drinking fresh apple cider and feeding bits of funnel cake to both dogs. Mark and Joey seemed to have entered a truce, and occasionally bits of sweetness between them popped up, which was lovely to see.

By the time we were finished the van was crowded, leaving only a small area for the dogs behind the net, and we were all exhausted. Our last stop was a farm market table where we bought a huge chicken pot pie and a bunch of side dishes. Joey, Mark and Brody joined us at our house to eat, and while the feast heated up we sprawled in the living room with the dogs around us.

Joey looked around, surveying the high ceiling in the living room, the layout of the furniture, the sliding glass doors that led out to the patio. "You've got a nice house here," he said. "Since My dad has been sick, he's been talking a lot about wanting to see me and Mark settled, in a house of our own."

"Don't you own the building where the antique store is, Mark?"

"I do. But I got a great deal on some Christmas stuff a few months ago, and that took over the second bedroom. Joey and I are feeling pretty crammed, and despite his small stature, Brody takes up a lot of space."

"He does not," Joey protested halfheartedly. He reached down to pet Brody's snowy-white head. "He hardly takes up any space at all."

"Except when he takes over the bed," Mark said. He spread his arms and legs out wide, in a mimicry of doggie behavior I knew very well.

Joey ignored him. "My dad knows that we're cooped up in the rooms above the store, and he's offered to give me and Mark a down payment on a house with more room, and a yard for Brody," Joey said.

I looked at Mark, whose face was dark. Was he happy enough above the store, and didn't want to move? Was he resentful that Joe Senior was pushing forward an idea that should have grown up organically between himself and Joey?

There were many reasons and I was sure I didn't know all of them. Maybe he wanted to keep himself financially untangled from Joey, for instance. It was possible that one of them had more debt than the other, or that Mark didn't want to be indebted to Joey's family.

Lili and I were committed to each other, but we had chosen not to marry, or change the deed on the townhouse, because we knew how complicated things could get if our emotions changed.

I considered myself very fortunate that my father had owned

his townhouse and left it to me in his will. Otherwise I'd never be able to own a house myself. "That's pretty generous of Joe Senior," I said.

"It is," Mark admitted. "And I don't want to sound ungrateful, but there are a lot of moving parts to consider if we're going to buy a place."

He leaned forward across the table, and I noticed that brought him closer to Joey. "I don't want to move too far away from the store, because I've spent a long time building my clientele and I don't want to set myself up for a big commute," he continued. "Stewart's Crossing is a pricey town, and the only way we can afford something is to get a fixer-upper." His body language relaxed then. "Fortunately, Joey is the handiest guy I know."

"You're sweet," Joey said, and I loved the look that passed between them.

"What would you think about River Bend?" I asked. "I met a guy recently who needs to sell his mother's house, and apparently it needs a lot of work."

Joey and Mark shared a glance. "You think we can look at it?" Joey said.

I didn't have Drew Greenbaum's phone number, but I knew the address. "Why don't we walk over there after dinner? You can see the outside, at least, and if he's not home we'll leave him a note."

After we ate, and fed the dogs, the four of us went out with Brody and Rochester and walked up toward Drew Greenbaum's house on Trieste Way. Brody pulled forward eagerly on his leash, and Rochester tugged to stay up with him. Then Brody would stop to dawdle beside a bush, and Rochester would push forward in search of a special smell. I could only imagine how difficult it would be for one person to walk both of them.

Lights were on in inside Sylvia Greenbaum's house and an aged Lexus sat in the driveway, so I hoped that meant Drew was home. "Why don't I take the dogs back to our house so you guys can look," Lili said.

"Can you manage both of them?" Mark looked worried. "Brody pulls."

"I have crawled on my belly through war zones to get the right shot," Lili said. "I think I can handle two big dogs."

"Be careful, sweetheart," I said. When she started to speak again, I held up my hands. "I know, belly, war zones."

She laughed, took the leashes and started away. Brody stalled, looking back at his dads, but she tugged on him, and he followed. I walked up to the front door and rang the bell.

Sylvia Greenbaum's house was a single-family, unlike my townhouse, though it was also on a zero lot line. It was a two-story property with a two-car garage and narrow yard on each side.

Drew answered, looking haggard in a faded T-shirt and ragged shorts. Lilibet the corgi hovered behind Drew's legs, yipping nervously.

"Hey, Steve," Drew said. "What's up?"

I introduced Joey and Mark. "They're looking for a house, and willing to take on a fixer-upper," I said. "If you haven't sold already I thought maybe you could show them."

"Sure, come on in." He leaned down and scooped up Lilibet.

Joey put his hand out for Lilibet to sniff, and she licked it. "She's a sweetheart," Joey said.

"When she wants to be," Drew said, as he led us into the foyer. "Off to the right, that's the half bath. Not usable right now because there's something wrong with the toilet."

He frowned. "I'm afraid that's going to be the theme here. Every time something went wrong, my mom just ignored it, and I've got two left thumbs, and I don't have the ready cash to hire somebody to fix things up."

The great room was ahead of us, with a two-story vaulted ceiling. Looking up, I saw a water stain on an area of the popcorn ceiling. "Is there a leak?" I asked.

"There was, a few years ago. My mom was swift enough back then to get the roof tile replaced, but she never had the popcorn fixed."

The house was tastefully furnished, with a couple of faded sofas, a walnut china cabinet and a big dining room table with eight chairs. "We could have the whole Capodilupo family over for holiday dinners," Mark said.

"If you can convince my mom not to be the hostess all the time," Joey said.

Drew clearly recognized that Mark and Joey were a couple but didn't seem to care. He showed them the kitchen, where the dishwasher was broken, and the study beyond it that could be an additional bedroom.

We climbed the stairs to see the master bedroom, where a hole gaped in the wall beside the queen-sized bed. "Another plumbing problem," Drew said. "That's the master bath on the other side. Plumber had to rip out part of the wall to get access, and of course my mother never had the wall fixed."

We toured the other two bedrooms and the full bath on that floor. The carpet was worn and stained in parts, and the whole house needed to be painted. Most of what was wrong looked like Joey could manage fixing it himself, with a contractor called in if necessary.

Drew led us back downstairs. "What do you think?" he asked.

Mark and Joey looked at each other. "It's a great house," Mark said. "Are you selling it furnished?"

"I don't need these big pieces," Drew said. "I can make you a deal if you're interested."

"What are you looking for in terms of price?" Joey asked.

"I had a Realtor out yesterday. She said the market in River Bend is depressed, and properties are selling for significantly lower than comparables in other neighborhoods. And with all the problems, she said I ought to start at four hundred thousand. If I'm going to sell to you direct, without a Realtor, we could split the commission I'd have to pay."

I thought it sounded like a great deal, but I wasn't the one putting out the money. "How soon do you need a decision?" Joey asked.

"I have another offer, but significantly lower than I want," he said.

I figured that was from Earl Garner but didn't say anything. But that did remind me that the association had placed a lien on the property, and I asked about that.

"I spoke to a guy at Pennsylvania Properties who's looking into that," Drew said. "I might be able to get the amount reduced significantly. Right now it's at forty thousand, and he thinks I can get that cut in half." He blew out a deep breath. "My cousin is an attorney, and he says he'll represent me, if I need it. And he said that I don't actually have to pay off the lien before I sell—that it can be paid off at closing."

"That's good news," I said. "So you can sell to anyone."

We thanked him and walked out. "What did you think?" I asked as we headed back to my townhouse. The twilight air seemed magical, hiding all the landscaping problems and leaving the homes sheathed a glow of streetlamps and those tiny solar-powered lights along driveways.

"I can fix almost all that stuff myself," Joey said. "The only thing I'm worried about is that roof leak. We'd have to get an inspection to make sure it's been repaired properly. And that ceiling is too high to work from a ladder—I'd need to build a scaffold, and for that I'd need someone else to help."

He turned to Mark. "What about you, sweetheart?"

"It's a lot of space. A yard out back for Brody. Eventually I could make that first floor bedroom into my office, and we can remodel the store to get more selling space."

"I agree, it's a great house. We'll have to see how much my dad can come up with towards the down payment."

Mark took Joey's hand in his. "If he can give us ten percent—forty thousand – then I can take a small mortgage out on the store." Then Mark turned to me. "My grandmother left the building to me free and clear, and I'm sure I can get a loan on it. And we could rent out the apartment we're living in, which would pay the mortgage."

"Sounds like you guys need to check your numbers and then make an offer," I said. "It would be great to have you as neighbors. And I love the idea of you having a yard where I can bring Rochester for play dates."

"Why do you think the properties here are going for so much less than others nearby?" Mark asked, as we turned the corner onto Sarajevo Way. With a sudden blare, rap music blasted from the house I'd identified as one of the rental properties.

The music didn't seem to bother either Mark or Joey, who waited for my answer.

"Right now we've got a lot of small maintenance and landscaping issues. Maybe that's all it is, and once we get those taken care of the values will pop back up again. So this might be a terrific time to buy. And I know Drew wants to get rid of that house."

I hoped that everything would work out—for their relationship, their purchase, and the value of my townhouse, too.

21: At Risk

Monday morning dawned gray and cold. It was clear that Indian summer was over, and we were heading toward a gloomy fall and an even gloomier winter. As I drove up the winding road to Friar Lake, I followed a roofer's truck. A couple of tiles had come loose on the roof of the chapel and I was glad Joey was having them repaired.

I spent the first part of the morning on Friar Lake business—following up on emails, filling out forms and so on. Midway through the morning I got an email back from Oscar Panaccio. He was interested in seeing my townhouse – was I free that evening? I responded that I was and made plans for him to come over at seven.

Around noon Joey stopped by my office, looking very cheerful. He wore a cream colored fisherman's sweater over a pair of jeans, with his regular Eastern ball cap on his head, though this time turned forward.

"I took your advice." He leaned down and petted Rochester, then sat across from me. "Mark and I had a long talk last night, and we worked through a bunch of things that have been bothering us. We both felt so much better that we plunged right into crunching numbers to see what kind of house we can buy."

"That's great," I said. Rochester thought so, too; he stood up and nuzzled Joey's knee in congratulations.

"I talked to my parents and they can give me fifty thousand

bucks – out of my eventual inheritance, of course. We decided that we want to put down twenty percent, to avoid having to pay for private mortgage insurance. Mark applied online for a home equity line of credit for his half, and we'll use the rest of my money, and whatever we need to draw down on the loan to fund the renovations."

In the background I heard the roofers working, the sound of hammers and men calling requests back and forth.

Joey smiled. "We called Drew this morning and made him an offer, contingent on an inspection, and he accepted."

I reached across the desk and shook Joey's hand. "Congratulations."

He stood up. "Now I'd better get back to watching the roofers on the chapel. I hope the repairs Drew's mom had done were good—otherwise I may end up on the roof of that house with tiles myself."

After Joey left, I turned my attention back to the file I had downloaded from the HOA website, and the references to LLCs that my analysis program had found. I started reviewing each of those forms. In each case, the committee member in charge of the interview had registered who he or she was meeting with.

At first I got confused, because Earl Garner's name kept popping up. Was he the person doing the interviewing? Then I realized no, he was the person behind twelve of those LLCs. Kimberly Eccles, also a member of the design committee, owned six of them. Three on her own and another three in joint tenancy with her husband. Oscar Panaccio owned five, which was a pretty nice clutch of properties for a guy living on a college professor's salary.

None of the other members of the board, or the design committee, owned multiple properties. However it was possible that they were still involved in the scheme somehow, perhaps by investing money with Garner, Eccles or Panaccio.

It wasn't illegal to buy properties, but there was definitely a moral gray area if members of the board of directors were deliberately driving down prices so that they could buy those homes at budget prices.

Of course, they were also keeping the price down for their own homes, but I assumed that at some point they would decide to bring River Bend back to its previous glory, and then prices would rise accordingly, and they could make a killing, property by property.

In the background I heard the roofers retracting the bucket lift they had used to access the high roof on the chapel. I was glad that the money to pay them came out of Joey's budget and not my own. I had enough to handle with advertising and paying people to support the conferences, like maids and caterers. Which reminded me that I needed to focus on my job for a while.

Though it was hard, I pushed away my research and focused on the job that paid my bills. Since real estate prices were on my mind, I wondered if I could bring in one or more of the Realtors who had spoken at the recent lunch. Real estate trends? Real estate as an investment? I brainstormed a bunch of ideas and then let them percolate for a while as I returned to my review of the data from River Bend's HOA.

A man named Jose Villanueva owned eight properties, and I realized that he lived across the street from Earl Garner. All of them were in joint tenancy with his wife, Daniela. On one, though, she had used her full name—Daniela Garner Villanueva.

That couldn't be a coincidence. She had to be a relative of Earl's. The remaining properties were all owned by individuals who either lived in the house or showed a personal address elsewhere.

Earl Garner was clearly taking advantage of the reduction in property values in River Bend to swoop up houses at bargain prices, and sharing that with his family member, and with Kimberly Eccles and Oscar Panaccio. It wasn't against the law to be a good businessman.

But as the president of the homeowner's association, Garner had a fiduciary duty to the community to keep up the property values. He, and the rest of the board, had the authority to maintain common areas, like our streets, our clubhouse and the pool. They also hired outside firms like the landscaping contractor.

Rochester was antsy, wandering around the office unable to settle, so I grabbed his leash and took him out. For the first time since early spring, I had to button up my jacket. Cold winds swept past Friar Lake's hilltop location, shaking the few remaining leaves from the deciduous trees.

Rochester didn't mind the weather; the golden retriever's double coat acted as an insulator, keeping him cool in the summer and warm in the winter. As we threaded our way along the sidewalks of Friar Lake, past the former monks' housing, renovated as modern dormitory rooms, I kept thinking about Earl Garner.

What if he, and other board members like Oscar Panaccio, were deliberately sabotaging our community to drive prices down and purchase neighborhood houses at a deep discount? Mortgage loans were at historically low rates, while rental rates were still high, so these buyers could probably make enough income to cover their mortgage debt and hold the properties for a few years. Then, when they were ready to sell, they could double down on improvements to River Bend, and voila, prices would shoot up.

Rochester spotted a pair of squirrels chasing each other up and down an oak tree, and he tugged forward because he wanted to play. While I held tight to his leash, I realized it was a clever scheme. Was it illegal? Hard to say, but Earl Garner was an attorney, so he might have found loopholes in the law that would prevent him and his cronies from being prosecuted.

What if Todd Chatzky knew about it, and with the new regulations that Pennsylvania Properties was going to institute, he was trying to combat the practice? Was that why his personality had changed from friendly to gruff?

Could that be a motive for one of the board members to kill him?

That was an idea I couldn't keep to myself. I led Rochester back to my office and called Rick. I got his voice mail, so left a message. "I have an idea I need to talk to you about. Call me as soon as you can."

My hand was shaking when I put down the phone. Was I living among murderers? And was my knowledge putting me and Lili at risk?

When we walked back into the gatehouse, Rochester sat on the floor, looking up at me. I got down on the floor with him, and he sprawled out beside me, his head in my lap. I stroked the soft down of his head and ears and willed myself to relax. As both Lili and Rick had warned me, I was jumping ahead of myself, imagining terrible scenarios based on the flimsiest of evidence.

After a few minutes of doggy love, I was ready to face the world again, and I jumped back into Friar Lake work, filling out yet another in a long line of requisition forms.

Rick called back an hour later. "I hope you have good news, because I've had a crappy day. More vandalism over the weekend – this time they hit the old mill, with graffiti and broken windows."

"Just the kind of thing your chief hates," I said. "I need to talk to you as soon as possible about the material I've been researching on Hi Neighbor, and some other stuff I've found out, because it's freaking me out. Can you meet me on my way home at the Chocolate Ear?"

"How about in an hour?" Rick asked. "I have a meeting with the chief of police in a couple of minutes. Probably have my ass handed to me, so I'll need some caffeine to recover."

I agreed and ended the call. I had investigated a number of crimes with Rochester in the past, but rarely had they hit as close to home as this one. I worried that one of my neighbors might be a murderer, and others crooks, and that Rochester and I weren't safe on our daily roams around the neighborhood. I had to figure this out, and soon.

22: Bucket Brigade

After a quick run through my email and outstanding issues, I locked up my office and headed for downtown Stewart's Crossing. A year earlier, Gail had expanded The Chocolate Ear into the space next door. She didn't offer table service there, so there were no restrictions against bringing your pet in with you. It was a great way to have Rochester accompany me and not have to sit outside.

When I got there, Rick was already inside at a table with a cup of coffee. "Been a long day," he said. "I'll watch Rochester while you get your coffee. Get me a piece of pastry while you're at it. Coffee's not enough, so I need some sugar, too."

I picked up a café mocha for myself, a pair of chocolate croissants, and one of Gail's dog biscuits, and brought them all back to the table. "So what's up?" Rick asked. "I hope it's good news, because I've had enough bad today."

"Well, I don't know if my news is good or bad for you, though it sounds bad for me." The volunteer fire alarm sounded, a high-low whoop that called our local residents to an emergency somewhere. As kids, we had learned the history of the department when a couple of volunteers came to our elementary school. We had heard about fighting fires, and been able to climb on the truck and try on helmets that were way too big for us.

"Can you imagine what it was like back in the day?" I asked Rick, when the alarm subsided. "When you had to bring your own bucket to the fire and they set up a chain of men to make a bucket brigade?"

That was a time when neighbors helped neighbors, I thought. Unlike today, when so many of my River Bend neighbors were complaining about each other and fighting, often to the detriment of the community.

"You remember that stuff, too?" Rick asked. "I'm surprised we still get by with a volunteer department, given how big the town has grown. Jerry Vickers belongs, you know. He's tried to get me to join a couple of times, but if I'm going to risk my life for a job I'd rather get paid for it."

Neither of us mentioned it, but there was the additional baggage of the fact that his ex-wife had left him for a firefighter. She'd left that guy, too, and a host of others, and though Rick was glad to be rid of her, he still had a soft spot in his heart for her.

He sipped his coffee. "So, what have you found?"

I reminded him that he'd noticed the number of complaints about renters at River Bend. "I got a list of all the rental properties from the association and started tracking ownership," I said, finessing how I'd gotten the list, or how I did the tracking.

"What did you find?"

"A couple of the board members have been snapping up houses and townhouses at bargain basement prices. I heard via a Realtor that prices are low compared to other areas because of all the maintenance problems at River Bend."

The fire truck zoomed past us on Main Street, siren going and lights flashing, and we had to wait for it to pass to talk again. Rochester squirmed under my chair, clearly bothered by the siren. There were only a couple of customers around us, including a woman with a rat terrier on her lap, but I didn't want to broadcast my business to everyone.

"What does that mean when it comes to murder of the property manager?"

"I don't know. But this could be a pretty profitable scheme, and it involves at least three of the board members, and a woman who I think is related to the board president. That doesn't sound right."

"I'd have to ask the district attorney if it's illegal, though," Rick said. "And that's a whole other crime than the one I'm investigating."

I reached down to pet Rochester, who had relaxed once the fire engine was gone. "Maybe not," I said. "At the design committee meeting the night he was killed, Todd Chatzky announced that there were changes coming to the way that Pennsylvania Properties managed the community. What if Todd figured out what was going on, and was trying to institute new rules that would prevent these guys from buying more properties?"

Rick looked skeptical.

"You always tell me there are four motives for murder. Love, lust, lucre and loathing. This operation sounds pretty lucrative, and if Todd threatened to stop it that could be a motive for getting him off the scene."

"Getting him fired or transferred, yeah," Rick said. "But knifing him in the gut seems over the top."

"I agree. But people act on impulse, too. Arguments get out of hand."

"They do, though not many people carry such a big knife around with them in case of an argument. I need a lot more evidence before I can make an arrest."

"Did you get anything more out of Todd's widow?"

"She remembered that she spoke with the security guard on duty as she was pulling out. I checked with him, and he verifies that it was around eight-thirty, because he had just come back from his break."

"How does that fit your timeline?"

"She insists that Todd was alive in the management office when she left. She says she saw a couple of men talking outside as she got into her car, but she didn't know who they were so there's no way to see if anyone saw her leave. The timeline is short— yes, she could have gotten her husband to take a walk with her, and stabbed him by the bench, but it's at the very opening of the window the ME came up with."

"How does she seem? Upset?"

"Steve. Her husband was just murdered. Of course she's upset. And it seems real to me, not something manufactured. I can't see her as viable suspect anymore, though I'm not clearing anyone at the present time."

"What about those men she saw? They were probably board members, hanging around after the design committee meeting. You could interview each of them, ask them if they were there after the meeting, if they saw her."

"You seem to forget I have some training and experience in this field," Rick said. "I've already done that. Oscar Panaccio and Earl Garner both confirmed they stayed in the parking lot after the meeting to talk about board business. Both say they went right home after that and didn't see Chatzky leave. Garner suggested that maybe Chatzky went out to look over one or more of the properties that were discussed at the meeting, and that someone, maybe a random mugger, approached him and killed him."

"A random mugger? In River Bend?" Could my disturbed dreams have been a prophecy?

"I don't give that much credence. He still had his wallet and keys on him. Despite the complaints I've heard River Bend has pretty good security, and it's doubtful someone with criminal intent could have managed to get in and be roaming around looking for a victim. Despite all the petty vandalism going on around town, we haven't had a crime against person like that for a long, long time."

He left soon after that, and I drove home with Rochester.

I walked and fed him, and Lili and I were just finishing dinner when the doorbell rang. Rochester began barking madly.

"Delivery?" Lili asked. "Seems kind of late."

I looked at my watch. "Oh, crap, I asked this guy from the board to come over and look at the house." It was tough to talk over Rochester's barking. "I'll tell you about it after he leaves. But I'm pretending that I might want to sell the house."

"You come up with the craziest schemes," she said, shaking her head. "You go, I'll clean up."

I grabbed Rochester by the collar as I opened the door to Oscar Panaccio. He looked a lot less formal than he had when I first met him at River Bend, in a Hawaiian shirt and board shorts, an outfit that looked way too young on a guy who had to be long past retirement.

"Thanks for coming over," I said, as I reached out to shake his hand. "This is Rochester. Don't worry, he's very friendly."

"The bigger question is how destructive he is," Oscar said. "He doesn't scratch the walls or stain the carpet, does he?"

I was insulted on Rochester's behalf, but I had to admit I knew people who complained about those problems from their dogs. "No, he's very good in that regard. Very well trained, and he goes to work with me most days, so he's not home alone much."

"You work at Eastern, don't you? You can bring a dog with you?"

"I've always had permission direct from President Babson," I said. "And at Friar Lake it's not an issue, because he stays inside whenever we have programming."

He nodded and looked around the living room. Lili stepped out of the kitchen then, and she stopped in surprise. "Dr. Panaccio," she said.

He looked over at her. "Dr. Weinstock. I didn't know you lived here in River Bend, too."

"I'm a fairly recent transplant. I moved in with Steve a couple of years ago." She smiled. "But we're both thinking of moving closer to Leighville to cut down on the commute. Traffic seems to get worse every year."

"I agree with that, but I'm committed to River Bend."

Rochester didn't seem to mind Oscar Panaccio; he sprawled on the living room floor as I showed Oscar the dining room, the breakfast nook and the kitchen. "Original cabinets and appliances," Oscar said. "They'll need to be replaced eventually."

Looking through his eyes, I noticed a couple of places where the white fiberboard had chipped on the corners and remembered the drawer beside the stove that you had to be careful with because it kept running off its track. "I did replace the garbage disposal last year."

"Hardly matters in terms of the price of the house," Oscar said. "Can I see the upstairs?"

Lili stayed downstairs with Rochester, and I led Oscar upstairs. Lili had hung pieces from her extensive collection of photographs along the stairway and in the upstairs hall. "Going to have to repaint after you take down all these pictures," Oscar said.

Like, duh, I wanted to say, but I resisted.

"Wallpaper in the bathrooms," he said, shaking his head. "I can see where the edges are curling. That's a pain to pull down."

I knew what his game was. He was picking out all the small problems so that he could come up with a low ball offer. But he didn't know I had no intention of selling.

After he'd finished criticizing the chips on the corner molding in the master bedroom and the original toilets in both bathrooms, he asked, "Whose name is on the deed? Yours alone?"

"Actually it's in the name of a trust my father created. I'm the beneficiary of the trust and I haven't changed the deed yet."

"You'll have to do that when you're ready to sell. How soon are you looking to get out of here?"

"Not sure. Like Lili said, the traffic is getting worse, and with all these problems in River Bend—the bad landscaping, the poor maintenance of the roads, and now Todd Chatzky's murder—well, it seems like the right time to leave."

"I'm prepared to make you an offer today," Oscar said. "Contingent on an inspection, of course. There could be a lot of hidden problems. How does two-fifty sound?"

I was surprised—first that a college professor had the kind of available resources to make a cash offer, and second because it was even lower than I had expected. "It sounds very low," I said. "Zillow says the property is worth at least three twenty-five."

"Zillow doesn't know what 's going on in this neighborhood," he said. "Like you said, there are a lot of problems unique to River Bend, and using comparables from outside the neighborhood won't work." He glared at me. "You're not trying to get a quote from Earl Garner, are you? Because I guarantee you he won't come close to my number."

"I hadn't thought of asking him. Is he buying houses too?"

"He has a nasty habit of snapping up properties before anyone else gets a chance," Oscar said. "Personally, I think he's using his position as board president to see which homeowners are in financial trouble, behind on their maintenance or racking up fines, and then swooping in on them like a vulture in a wheelchair."

An interesting image, for sure.

"Well, I don't think we're desperate enough to sell at such a discount," I said. "Maybe with a new property manager we'll see some improvements in the problems here and values will go back up. We'll hold on for a while, but I appreciate your coming over."

"Nothing's going to change as long as Garner is president," Oscar said. "Mark my words, property values are going to keep going down."

"Then why are you eager to buy?"

"Right now rental prices are holding steady, which means there's a good spread between mortgage payments and rental income."

"But I thought you were making a cash offer?"

"I am. I buy for cash, then take out a mortgage afterward so I can pull my cash back out for the next property."

"You sure you're not in the business department?" I asked, with a laugh.

"Just because I teach biology doesn't mean I have my head in the clouds," he said. "Anyway, my offer stands for the next week. Call me if you want to take advantage of it."

I walked him out and was surprised that Rochester remained on the floor in the living room. He must have trusted Oscar Panaccio, which was in his favor. Rochester was a good judge of character, and if he liked somebody, even someone who didn't pay him much attention, then despite Oscar's grumpiness I had to assume he wasn't a strong suspect in Todd Chatzky's death.

When I returned to Lili in the living room and sat in the recliner across from her, she asked, "What did he have to say?"

"Nit-picked every little problem," I said. "Useful information, though. If we stay here, we're going to have to redo the kitchen, you know. I noticed a lot of little chips in the cabinets, and he's right, these appliances are going to fail eventually."

"But we're not considering moving, are we? I just made up that bit about the traffic to support you."

"I caught that, and I appreciate it. We work well as a team." I smiled at her. "But no, I don't want to move anytime soon. With winter coming, Florida doesn't look that bad. I wouldn't love to leave my job at Eastern, but President Babson isn't going to live forever, and even if he says around, who knows what will happen to Friar Lake. Unless your mother's health gets worse and you want to move closer to her."

"Since you've never met my mother, you don't understand how

little I want to live close to her. Right now my brother's taking care of anything she needs, so we can stay here. And the cold weather will just require us to snuggle up more, right?"

In answer, Rochester jumped up on the couch beside her and rested his head on her lap. "Hey, that was my cue, dog," I protested.

23: Angle of Attack

That night I slept restlessly, dreaming about sirens and danger in the neighborhood, though there was no form to my fears. The next morning, Rochester was bugging me for a walk at sunrise. I didn't want to get up, but I knew he'd be relentless. I struggled out of bed and checked the temperature outside. For the first time since the spring, the thermometer had dipped below sixty in the morning. I added a light sweater to my T-shirt and jeans.

I have learned to trust my premonitions and fears, so I dug out the knife my father had left me and hooked it onto the belt of my jeans. When we walked outside I shivered, though I wasn't sure if it was from the chill or from the feelings that remained from my dreams.

We encountered no one dangerous, though. By the time we were walking back home, the sun had risen, and I pulled off my sweater and tied it around my waist. As we approached her single-story house, my friend Norah was pacing back and forth outside.

"Hey, Norah, what's up?" I asked, as Rochester tugged me toward her.

She pointed to the oak in front of her house, where one broken branch hung at a crazy angle over the sidewalk.

"This branch broke in the big wind the other day, and I've been after the association to come and cut it down. I'm worried someone might hurt themselves on the sidewalk and then come after me for leaving it hanging."

I looked at the branch. It was a big break, but still too connected to be twisted off. Then I remembered the knife at my belt. "Let me see if I can cut it off," I said. "Can you hold Rochester's leash for a minute?"

"Sure."

I handed her the leash and pulled the knife off my belt. As I slipped it out of the sheath Norah said, "That's a big knife. You could do some real damage with that."

I considered my angle of attack, and began sawing at the branch, cutting through the wood fibers.

"You know who else has a knife like that?" Norah asked. "Earl Garner. I should have asked him when I saw him yesterday, though I don't think he could have reached the branch from his chair."

I stopped cutting. "Garner has a knife like this?"

"Sure. He has it attached to the side of his chair. He said he uses it if something gets stuck in one of his wheels."

Garner had a knife, I thought, as I went back to the tree. He could have used it to kill Todd Chatzky. I had to tell Rick, and see if the angle of the blade's entry could match someone in a wheelchair. And would there have been a lot of blood in that case?

But first I had to finish cutting this damn branch. The last fibers were from the outside of the branch, and they resisted. I finally put the knife aside and grabbed one end of the branch and tugged.

It broke, with a satisfying crack that made Rochester look up. "Here you go," I said. I tossed it on the ground beside the tree, back from the sidewalk. "The landscape people should pick it up when they come by next."

"I'm not going to wait," Norah said. "Thank you so much. I'm going to drag it over to the common area by the lake. Let it be someone else's problem."

"That's one way to handle it." I took Rochester's leash back from her and she grabbed the branch by the end I'd cut. She started tugging it down the street as Rochester and I headed for home.

It was still early by the time we got back, so I texted Rick. "More ideas. Café in an hour?"

I was feeding Rochester when my phone pinged with single letter K.

"When did it get so hard to type two letters instead of one?" I grumbled.

Lili came down as I was making breakfast, and I scrambled a couple of eggs for her while she made toast. I didn't want her to worry about why I was carrying a knife on my walk with Rochester, so I didn't say anything, other than I was meeting Rick for coffee at the Chocolate Ear on my way to work.

"Twice in two days?" she asked. "Are you helping him with the murder?" She looked at me. "Of course. Why would I even ask?" She started clearing the dishes. "Does this have to do with why you invited Professor Panaccio over last night? Are you considering him a suspect?"

I stood up to help her and explained what I had found. Then I hurried through a shower and loaded Rochester in the car. This time I got to the café before Rick, and I was settled with two cups of mocha and two chocolate croissants when he came in.

"You look like you're ready for business," he said, as he sat across from me. He scratched Rochester, then picked up one of the coffee cups. "Shoot."

I explained about cutting the branch for Norah, and how she mentioned that Earl Garner had a knife like mine. "Can you get a search warrant for his house?" I asked. "See if you can match the knife to Todd Chatzky's wounds?"

"Hold on, cowboy. I can't randomly get a warrant for someone's house on the word of a neighbor that he has a knife that might match the weapon we're looking for."

"But we talked about motive last night," I protested. "This information adds to it."

"Still not enough." Rick took a bite of his croissant. "Thanks for the food and the coffee, though."

I wasn't going to stop so easily. "Did you find out anything from the ME about the angle of the knife thrust? Could it have come from someone in a wheelchair?"

"He did say that there was an upward thrust to the angle of the knife cuts, which implied someone who was shorter than Mr. Chatzky."

"Can you ask if it's reasonable that a man in a wheelchair could have delivered them? From what I've seen Earl Garner has a lot of upper body strength."

"I'm having a hard time thinking a guy in a wheelchair could do this," Rick said. "Remember, Chatzky's body was found between a bench and a hedge. How could Garner drag the body there? The physics don't work."

I thought back to the crime scene. "What if Todd and Garner were arguing, and Todd tried to get away? Maybe he got behind the bench to put some space between him and the wheelchair."

"Why didn't he just run?"

"I've seen Garner in his chair, playing catch with his son. He can really move. I'll bet he could have outrun Todd."

Rick frowned. "But he could have run across the grass, and the chair couldn't have followed."

I shook my head. "There's no grass close to where the body was found. It's all pavement. And there are no houses nearby, so even if Todd was screaming for help no one might have heard him."

I closed my eyes and visualized the scene. "Todd's behind the bench, and he and Garner are arguing. Garner realizes that his scheme is going to fall apart, and he gets desperate. Pulls the knife from his wheelchair, corners Todd, and sticks the knife in his gut. As Todd falls behind the bench, Garner pulls the knife out of him and rolls away."

"It's a possibility," Rick said. "Not as big a leap as some of your deductions."

"So you'll check it out?"

"I'll ask the ME."

I had to get up to Friar Lake, so Rochester and I left Rick finishing his coffee. I had a slew of requisition forms to fill out for upcoming programs, and I spent the morning doing that. After a quick lunch and run around the property with Rochester, I sat down to consider the real estate program I'd thought about the day before.

How could I focus it in a way that would bring in alumni who weren't local to Leighville or its environs, who weren't interested in selling their homes at the present? Buying and renting residential property as an investment strategy, the way that Oscar Panaccio was doing? The stock market was jittery, and home mortgage rates were on the rise making it harder for new home buyers to get in. Was this a good time to leverage your capital into property?

I went through the business cards I'd picked up at the lunch the previous week. I did a quick run through our alumni database and discovered two Realtors who had degrees from Eastern.

From the photo on her business card, I recognized the woman who had raised the question about new communities without HOAs, and the buyers she had who were interested in those places. Maybe that meant she had some clients buying for investment purposes. Her Eastern connection, though, made her the best bet to start, and I called her.

She answered her phone with her name. "Faith Magyar. How can I help you?"

I explained who I was and how I had heard her speak at the

lunch. "I live in River Bend, in Stewart's Crossing, and several of my neighbors have been buying up homes and renting them out. That made me think about organizing a program on buying and renting residential property as an investment strategy, and I wondered if you'd be interested in facilitating a program like that. Since you're an Eastern alum, you know the kind of people you'd be speaking to, and it might be an opportunity for you to meet potential investors or at least get your name out as an expert."

"I'd love to," she said. "I have a couple of Canadian clients right now who are looking for investment properties, so I've been digging around in that area for a while. I'm interested that you mentioned River Bend—I haven't seen any new listings there in a while, which is surprising. A community that size usually has at least ten active listings. But if neighbors are buying up properties before they go on the market, that explains it. It's also bad for values because you don't allow the market to set the price."

We brainstormed a couple of ideas and potential dates, and she said she'd get back to me with a confirmation in the next couple of days.

That afternoon, I left Friar Lake right after Joey, Rigoberto and Juan did, and returned to River Bend. I took Rochester out for his walk early, and as we passed Earl Garner's street I saw him outside, watering his landscaping from his wheelchair. Rochester tugged me forward down that street, and I followed his lead. I wanted to get a closer look at Garner's wheelchair and see if I could spot the knife Norah had mentioned.

"Good afternoon," I said, as we approached him. "Steve Levitan. Thanks for helping me out at the design committee meeting last week."

"I don't help people out, I just follow the rules," he said.

"Surely you can bend those now and then," I said. "Look at poor Drew Greenbaum. He just wants to get his mother's house sold. If the association can drop some of those liens, he can get a better price and a quicker sale."

I could only see the left side of his chair from my position, and from the way he held the hose it looked like he was right-handed.

"I've already made him an offer and promised to take care of the liens if he accepts," he said. "That's the best that I can do."

Rochester sniffed the base of a tree on the other side of Garner's property and lifted his leg against it. Then he tried to get closer to where Garner was watering, but I held him back. "That isn't fair, is it? You'll only help him with the liens if you can buy the property?"

"What's it to you?"

"I care about the way this community is being run. I want to see the roads repaired, better control of the landscape company, and property values going up. I hope the new property manager will be able to turn things around."

"If you really care, then run for the board," Garner said.

I kept waiting for him to turn his chair around so I could see the other side, but he didn't move.

"I might. But right now I want to know why things have been going wrong. There's something wrong with the way the board is run, but I'll bet you won't be able to run over the new property manager so easily."

He glared at me, and Rochester moved in front of me to protect me.

"Don't you care what happened to Todd Chatzky?" I demanded. "He was killed right here, in River Bend. Doesn't that make you want to find out how and why?"

"I don't mess with police business, and you shouldn't either."

"If you ran the board better, I wouldn't have to," I said.

He shut off his hose and rolled his chair back up to his garage. He kept the left side toward me, so I couldn't see if he kept a knife on the right side. A moment later he was inside, and the door was coming down.

"Well, I guess he told us," I said to Rochester.

24: Judge of Character

I was shaken by my confrontation with Earl Garner. I had gotten a hostile vibe from him, and so had Rochester, from the way my sweet dog demonstrated he wanted to protect me from the man in the wheelchair. I was worrying about that as I drove up to River Bend. The morning chill had worn off, and I drove with the windows open. Rochester kept his head out, his snout forward to sniff everything that came his way.

My day went downhill from there. One of the professors I counted on to do a bunch of presentations for me had gotten approved for a sabbatical in the winter term, and he was going to be too busy to do the program he had scheduled with me for November, and out of town for the one in February.

A group that had planned to rent out Friar Lake for a big conference in January had changed its plans with the death of the featured speaker. And another smaller group cancelled a Saturday event, too.

It was looking like my revenue projections were crumbling. What would happen if I couldn't make a go of the center? I knew President Babson would cut me some slack, because Friar Lake was his pet project. But how long could he manage that?

I struggled through the afternoon, but it was hard to concentrate when I was so worried. It was a relief to leave Friar Lake and its problems behind, but after dinner and Rochester's evening walk, I remembered I had another problem on my hands.

What was going on at River Bend?

I opened my laptop and put in Earl Garner's name, because I wanted to know more about his background and see if he was capable of cheating our whole community—and of killing Todd Chatzky. I discovered that there was a lot more to the story of his paralysis than I had originally heard.

Yes, he was riding his bike during his second year in law school when he was run over. What Eric Hoenigman hadn't known, or hadn't told me, was where and when the accident had happened. After reading a series of articles in the *Philadelphia Inquirer* I had a clearer picture.

Garner originally stated that he was riding home from the Temple University law library on his bicycle late one evening and got lost, ending up about a dozen blocks north of the campus, near the intersection of North Broad Street and West Erie Avenue. Around two AM, a white van with its headlights off hit him, throwing him to the ground.

Police detectives were suspicious. The accident scene was about two miles from Garner's apartment near the law school, and Garner's excuse, that he'd been focusing on a case he was studying, didn't make sense to them.

His detour had taken him to an area of North Philadelphia known as the Badlands, notorious for drug deals, and police subpoenaed Garner's blood while he was in the hospital. It showed traces of crystal meth in his system. Eventually Garner confessed to having ridden up to the Badlands to score some methamphetamine to help him through his exams. He gave the police information on the dealer he had bought from, and said that he was on his way home to sleep when he was hit.

The dealer, when eventually apprehended, had a different story. Earl Garner had grabbed a baggie of ice, the smokable form of crystal meth, and taken off on his bike without paying. The dealer had jumped into his van and chased after him, running him off the road. He had retrieved his drugs and left Garner where he had fallen.

It was an awful story, and I had to sit back and take it all in. Rochester came over to me and slumped on the floor, and I got down there and petted him.

On the one hand, I admired Earl Garner, because he had managed to overcome his addiction while in the hospital and in rehab. He had never been charged with a crime, so he was able to return to Temple, finish his degree, and set up his own practice in Stewart's Crossing.

But on the other hand, knowing more about his background made me trust him even less. He had been an addict and a thief, and the fact that he'd never been charged, and been able to pass the bar, didn't change that.

Then again, I had been convicted of a felony myself and imprisoned for a year. Like Earl Garner, I had fought back to create a new life for myself. I ought to feel more empathy for him, but I didn't, and I wondered why.

The evidence of my recovery was all around me. The golden retriever knickknacks on the bookcase testified to the new life I had begun when Rochester came into my life. The framed photos on the walls, some of them Lili's, others she had collected, were evidence of my ability to keep growing and open up to love with her.

Earl Garner had a wife, a son he played ball in the street with. He'd started over again, too. But what if he was hiding dark secrets? I was; the fact that I occasionally used my hacker laptop up in the attic was evidence of that.

I opened a new browser window and looked for information on Garner's law practice. Its address was in the same co-working space where my attorney, Hunter Thirkell, had his office. Did they know each other?

Before I could second-guess myself I grabbed my cell phone and dialed Hunter's number. I hadn't spoken to him for a few months, since I had helped him prove the innocence of one of his clients. "Hey, Steve. Hope you're not in trouble again."

"Nope. Just doing a little research on something that's going on here in River Bend. The president of our association's board of directors is an attorney, and he's in the same building you are. You know Earl Garner?"

"I know he's a jerk," Hunter said. That was one thing I liked about him—he pulled no punches when he didn't like someone. "Never says hello when I see him in the hallway. And just last week that wheelchair of his was leaking oil and it left a nasty spill in the conference room. He didn't even bother to tell the receptionist so she could get it cleaned up."

Something about that comment resonated with me but I pushed the thought aside to come back to it later. "Any idea how his business is doing?"

"I know he has a lot of bar complaints against him right now," Hunter said. "One client has documented six instances where Garner failed to communicate important information in a timely manner. He does a lot of contingency work and apparently he fails to follow through on things like evidence requests. And he's also a licensed real estate broker, and he's been accused a few times of mingling escrow funds with his business accounts, and failing to disburse them quickly."

"Wow."

"Don't get excited, though. He's a sole practitioner and his paralegal is as dumb as a box of rocks, so most of it is probably negligence rather than criminal activity. Why are you interested in him?"

I gave Hunter a quick rundown of what was going on at River Bend. "I think he and the rest of the board are conspiring to keep the community in poor shape so that they can snap up properties at bargain prices."

"That sounds like a breach of fiduciary duty to me," Hunter

said. "That's not a crime in most jurisdictions, but it can lead to civil liability, and in some cases the situation that causes the breach is related to criminal activity."

I thanked Hunter for his information, and walked upstairs, Rochester trailing behind me. Lili was in the office, typing away at the computer, and I leaned in the doorway and watched her. "What's up?" she asked, when she finished what she was doing and looked my way. "You look like you've seen a ghost."

"I did some research into Earl Garner's past and it freaked me out." I told her what I had found. "I feel like I ought to be able to put all that aside and admire him for overcoming those obstacles, getting his life back on track."

"Like you did."

"Like I did. But I can't."

"Why do you think you can't?"

"I don't know," I said, and I could hear something agonized in my voice. "He was never even convicted of a crime, and arguably he suffered a worse penalty than I did."

"What does Rochester think about him?"

I cocked my head.

"You're always saying the dog is such a good judge of character. Has he seen Garner?"

Rochester knew we were talking about him, and he sat on his hind legs beside me and nuzzled my hand.

"Earlier this evening." I described the way my conversation with Garner had devolved into an argument, and Rochester's reaction. "It seemed like he wanted to protect me, the way he stepped in front of me."

"There you go. Rochester doesn't like him, so you don't either, despite any logical attempt you might make to feel sympathetic toward him."

"Part of the argument was my fault," I said. "I egged him on."

"Which you did before you knew the full story behind his paralysis. Ergo, you already decided that he's not a good guy, and even what you learned this evening hasn't changed that opinion."

"I love it when you use logic on me," I said, smiling.

"Ergo, you need something to take your mind off all these problems." She pushed her chair back from the computer and stood up. "I know what that is."

25: Data Points

Thursday morning as I prepared to take Rochester for his walk, I was still thinking about my conversation with Earl Garner the day before. We'd have to avoid his street on our way around the lake. I didn't want him to try and run us over.

Then I remembered the marks on the sidewalk I saw the day after the murder. Maybe they hadn't been made by the lawn service – could they have been made by the wheels on Earl Garner's chair? I remembered what Hunter had said about Garner's wheelchair leaking oil. Hadn't I seen some spilled liquid near Todd's body? What if that had been oil as well as blood?

I grabbed a tape measure from the kitchen drawer and pulled on my jeans, T-shirt and sweater. It was cooler than it had been the day before, and goose bumps rose on my arms as a breeze swept past us, stirring the last dead leaves along Sarajevo Court.

Rochester seemed to know we were on a mission, and instead of dallying to sniff every tree and pile of leaves, he pulled forward toward the twin lakes. We turned onto River Bend Drive and waved as we passed Norah, outside surveying her landscaping and shaking her head.

As we approached the ramp that led to the sidewalk between the lakes, I saw the faded marks I had noticed the day after Todd's murder when Rochester strained to sniff something, almost knocking me over in his eagerness.

I turned to look and saw him sniffing at a dark green block that resembled a chunk of the dental chews I gave him – a rectangle about an inch long, with three square blocks sticking up from it.

But those weren't dental chews. We'd had a rat problem in one of the buildings at Friar Lake the previous winter, and Joey had brought in a tub of rat poison to put out. That green block, and another a few feet away, had come from a tub like the one Joey had bought.

Was that just sloppiness by the exterminator? Or had someone deliberately put the poison there to kill someone's dog—or perhaps keep nosy dog owners on the move?

I tugged Rochester back, and took my phone out. I snapped a couple of pictures and inserted them into an email them to Lois, Todd's secretary. "I'm going to throw these away, but you should have the maintenance guy look around the property in case there are more, before a dog or cat gets sick," I added, and clicked send.

I grabbed one of the plastic bags from the dog waste station and used it to pick up the block, careful not to get my fingerprints on it.

I didn't want to hang around near the oily marks because I wanted to get Rochester away from that rat poison, so I gave up on trying to measure the marks on the sidewalk. We hurried through the traffic circle on River Bend Drive, and as soon as we crossed, he sniffed a spot along the hedge and did his business. Our walk home was more leisurely, Rochester stopping to sniff and pee, as if his work for the day was done and he could relax.

My work had only begun, though. Lili and I had breakfast and I fed Rochester, and then the dog and I drove up to Friar Lake. It was nine o'clock when I got there, and I called Lois to make sure she'd gotten my email. "That's not the kind of poison our exterminator uses," she said. "I've never seen those. Are you sure they're poisonous?"

"I am. I'll send you the link to the product on Amazon."

"I'll get someone out to look around, just to be safe," she said.

"But if you could send me the link I'd appreciate it."

I opened a browser on my computer, found the product online, and then sent the link to Lois. Then I sat back to consider. What had Rick discovered about the angle of the fatal wounds to Todd Chatzky? If they couldn't have come from a man in a wheelchair, I was barking up the wrong tree.

"Any word back from the ME?" I asked, when Rick answered his phone.

"And good morning to you," Rick said. "Hey, Steve, how's your week going? Because mine is crap."

I took a deep breath. "Sorry. I have a couple of ideas to run past you, and I was too eager. You having more vandalism problems?"

"Nothing new. But the chief is chewing my ass looking for results and I don't have any."

"Do you think you could come over to my place after work? Bring Rascal and the dogs can have a play date. I want to show you a piece of rat poison I found this morning."

"Rat poison?"

"It was near where Todd's body was found. I picked it up using a doggie waste bag so I wouldn't get my prints on it."

"And let me guess. You want me to check it for fingerprints."

"Only if it's relevant. To sweeten the deal, I've got some new Dogfish Head Liquid Truth Serum IPA we can break open. I'll even throw in a pizza."

"You had me at beer, but pizza's even better."

I met with Joey that morning to go over the schedule of upcoming programs and review any maintenance issues that might affect them. Then he ducked out to meet with the inspector reviewing Drew Greenbaum's mother's house. I spent the afternoon on paperwork and emails, the bane of any administrator's existence.

Joey texted me late in the afternoon, that the inspector hadn't found any major problems, and he and Mark were going to be able to buy the house.

"Welcome to the neighborhood," I texted back. I was excited to have one of Rochester's playmates close by, and to take advantage of the yard that came with the Greenbaum house.

Before I left work, I ordered a pizza from Giovanni's, in the shopping center in downtown Stewart's Crossing. Rick and I both liked the same kind—a thick crust with spicy Italian sausage crumbled and scattered over a base of homemade tomato sauce, freshly sautéed mushrooms and shredded mozzarella from an artisan cheese maker in New Hope. We'd converted Lili, Tamsen and Justin into believers, too.

Because there would be three humans and two dogs for dinner, I added a half-dozen garlic rolls and a small blue cheese salad to the order. I stopped on the way home to pick it up and stow it in the trunk. Rochester hopped from the front seat to the back, sniffing and grumbling as he realized he couldn't get into the trunk.

"You'll get yours when we get home, dog," I said. "Now chill out."

I caught his face in the rear view mirror, a mask of sadness, and he slumped down onto the seat. I couldn't help laughing.

Rick and Rascal arrived a few minutes after I got home, and we all sat down to eat. "Good news on the vandalism front," Rick said. "Late last night we got lucky and caught three teenaged boys spray-painting four-letter words on the windows of the laundromat. Spray paint they were using matches the kind used on the other incidents, and we leaned on them and got them to cop to a couple of other incidents, and finger some other kids who've been causing trouble."

"Your chief must be happy about that."

"He'll be happier if we nail down some convictions, and we see the activities stop."

"Did they give you any reason for their actions?" Lili asked.

"Teenaged angst? Or something more?"

"Typical stories. Too much time on their hands, too much anger on social media, parents not paying attention. One of the kids even lives here in River Bend, and he tried to put a spin on his actions like nobody cares about the environment, climate change and all that, so why not have some fun destroying things?"

I shook my head. "It's one part of your broken windows theory in action. Kids see no one cares about the area around them so they're not motivated to stay out of trouble."

Between their own chow and pizza crusts, both dogs were fat and happy by the time we were finished.

"I'll clean up so you guys can talk," Lili said, and Rick and I went into the living room. I told him about my confrontation with Earl Garner the day before, and how Rochester had tried to protect me.

"I wish you wouldn't keep pushing the boundaries," Rick said. "You've gotten yourself in danger in the past. You don't seem to learn from your mistakes."

"Ooh, I had an argument with a man in a wheelchair," I said. "Big danger."

"A man you think killed someone. Don't mess around, Steve."

He was serious, and I knew that and believed him. He took notes in his leather-bound notebook as I continued, through the details of Garner's addiction and his accident.

"It's all interesting," Rick said. "But as you know yourself, one criminal problem doesn't make someone a lifetime villain. And it's a big jump from stealing a baggie of crystal meth from a dealer to sticking a knife in someone's belly."

"There's one more thing." I explained about the marks I had seen on the pavement the day after Todd's death.

"I saw those, too. Puddle of oil, probably from a lawnmower idling there, then the mower runs through them."

"That's what I thought at first," I said. "But what if those tracks match Earl Garner's wheelchair? That puts him at the scene of the crime."

"It's been over a week since the murder. Doubtful that any traces of that oil are still on Garner's wheelchair wheels."

"But we could go out and measure the marks, and see if they match a lawnmower, or a chair. It's another piece of evidence. I tried to do that this morning but got distracted by the rat poison. Which, by the way."

I got up and found the plastic doggie bag with the poison inside. "It's here by the door when you're ready to leave."

He sighed. "We can walk over there. You have a flashlight?"

"I have a dog who needs walking in the dark," I said. "I've got at least three."

The lights I had were tiny, high-intensity ones that slipped easily into a pocket or onto a leash. I handed one to Rick and took one for myself, and we left the dogs behind as we walked out.

"Do you think Garner killed Chatzky?" Rick asked.

"I do. My hypothesis, which is a nicer word than guess, is that Todd reported the way Garner has let the board run down the community, allowing him to buy up properties at bargain rates. And that conference call he was on the night of his murder was about some changes that Pennsylvania Properties wants to make, or maybe even the management company planning to challenge the board."

"But doesn't letting the community run down lower the value of the properties that Garner and the other board members own?"

"It's a long game," I said. "Max out his ability to buy property, then turn around the community and the values go back up. Steady income from the renters while he holds the properties, then big gains once he resells them."

"Why don't the other board members complain?"

I shrugged. "I don't know. Some of the ones I've read about on Hi Neighbor are there for only one issue. A woman who wants to prevent the board from converting one of the empty lots into a playground. A man who's opposed to setting up reserves for new roofs for the townhouses, to avoid an assessment eventually. If Garner and his cronies go along with them, maybe they go along with Garner."

The streets of River Bend were quiet as we walked up to the twin lakes, only a couple of cars passing, the distant sound of a kid practicing the first movement of Mozart's "A Little Night Music" on the piano. It was one of the first songs I had learned when I began studying, the metronome ticking on the piano above me, and I'm sure my parents were fed up with my efforts by the time I mastered it.

We stopped at the ramp where the puddle of oil had been, which was now just a fading stain. Then we followed the tracks, which petered out a few feet from the place where I had found Todd's body.

I took out a measuring tape and while Rick held a flashlight, I measured the width of the tires that had made the marks, and the distance between them. Rick wrote them down in his notebook.

"What do you think?" I asked, when I stood up. I was excited, like Rochester when he found a rubber ball that had been hidden behind a piece of furniture.

"I think we need to compare these measurements to standard wheelchairs."

"Party pooper," I said.

"It's called logical thinking. You should try it sometime."

I snorted, and we walked back to the townhouse under a canopy of stars surrounded by the chirping of crickets. Rick and I sat at the dining room table and looked at wheelchairs. "That looks like the one Garner uses," I said, pointing at a lightweight chair with large wheels.

We compared the measurements we had taken, and concluded that the ruts looked the right size for a wheelchair. "The wheel marks are too close together for a riding mower," I said. "Or for one of those stand-on mowers the landscapers use here."

Rick agreed with me. "But it's still all circumstantial. The details are good, but I'll need something more concrete than your dog feeling threatened before I can bring Garner in for questioning."

"We have so much data already," I said. "Why isn't that enough?" I started enumerating. "Garner had a motive: he needs to protect his real estate empire, and Todd was threatening that."

"Evidence for that point?" he asked me.

I reiterated Todd's speech about things changing at River Bend the night of the design committee meeting, but Rick shook his head. "Too vague."

I frowned but continued. "Means. My friend Norah told me that Garner owns a knife like the one the evidence points to was used on Todd Chatzky."

"So do you, and about a thousand other people in the area."

"Opportunity. Garner was hanging around after the meeting. He could have argued with Todd and gone after him with his knife."

"Could being the operative word there."

"But you have all three elements," I said. "Isn't that enough to bring him in for questioning?"

Rick blew out a big breath. "I'll have a tech examine the rat poison for fingerprints, and I'll lay this out for my chief they way you have. If he agrees, I'll bring Garner in. But no guarantees. He may see this evidence as even flimsier than I do."

26: Messenger Bag

I spent most of Friday morning on the phone with Epiphania, who had agreed to bring her next meeting of the La Leche League to Friar Lake that afternoon. She had a dozen questions, and even though I'd answered them all before, she kept asking. Was I sure there would be enough parking? How far was the ladies' room from the meeting site? How many tables would there be where women could spread out their baby paraphernalia and change diapers if necessary?

In between calls, I leaned down to Rochester. "Next time I want to offer Friar Lake to a neighbor, please bark or growl or something."

He opened his mouth in a big doggy grin as if to say, "You're the dumb human who invited her."

I prepared a quick flyer introducing Friar Lake and offering our meeting rooms for corporate events and community groups, and added directions to the rest rooms at the bottom. When the large classroom was renovated, it had been furnished with rows of tables perfect for diapers, bottles and educational toys – though I was sure the monks were shuddering somewhere at the way I was using it. I even made sure that both the bathrooms were clean and well-stocked.

The mothers and babies began arriving at 11:45. I left Rochester in my office and stood in the parking lot, where I directed them down the sidewalk to the classroom building. The babies were adorable, which made me happy and sad at the same time. I wanted to pick each one up, kiss their delicate heads, make them smile and gurgle. But at the same time I knew that was some last-ditch atavistic desire toward fatherhood, which had been dealt out of the cards for me years before.

I didn't sit in on their meeting. Don't get me wrong, I'm a big fan of breasts. But I didn't want to see a few dozen of them all at once, and I didn't want to intrude on the mothers' privacy.

Instead, I sat in my office and answered emails until Rick called. "It's going to take a day to get someone to search the databases for fingerprints on that block of rat poison. I met with the chief this morning, and he thinks all the evidence is circumstantial, which it is. He doesn't think the DA will give me a search warrant for Earl Garner's home and the HOA office until we have something more definitive."

"Crap."

"There's something more. You know Garner is an attorney, right? He has sued a bunch of towns and townships over handicap access to public buildings. Including a suit against Stewart's Crossing that required our department to change the angle of the access ramp that leads to our front door and relocate the button that opens the door. A lot of other stuff, too, which cost the department and town a lot of money. I think the chief is scared that if we go after him and he's innocent, he'll come back after us again."

"I'm sure the town wouldn't have made the changes if the law didn't require them."

"I know that, and I'm not saying we shouldn't have open access to all citizens. But he's a nitpicker and so I have to move very carefully."

The La Leche League meeting broke up soon after that. The mothers were friendly and grateful, and I led a group of a half-dozen of them around the winding paths, pointing out the old stone buildings and how we had repurposed them. "This is such a beautiful place," one of the women said. "So nurturing. I hope we can come back here often."

If you can get someone other than Epiphania to be my contact, I thought. But I smiled and said, "We're here to serve the community."

I stood outside the gatehouse and waved goodbye as the last cars left. Those moms were so attentive to their kids, and I wondered how long that would last. Supposedly breast-feeding increased the bond between mother and child. But when those kids grew up to be teenagers, would the bond still be strong? Would these moms, and the dads involved, still pay so much attention to their kids then, keeping them out of trouble?

I was in a melancholy mood that afternoon, and Rochester sensed that and curled up around my legs. I thought about how lucky those moms were to have children.

When Mary remarried and gave birth to a healthy baby, I had terrible mixed emotions. I still cared for her, despite all we had been through, and I was happy that she'd been able to have the child she wanted so much. But I was angry and jealous, too. Why couldn't that baby have been mine? I was sure that could have been a good father. I had a good role model in my own dad.

But it wasn't to be. By then I was in my late thirties, and I couldn't start to date again, no less get married and try once more for a family. It wasn't until Rochester came into my life that my heart began to open once more. And then I met Lili, who was a bit older than I was, and neither of us were eager to start a family.

Time kept slipping away, and when Lili turned forty we acknowledged that we were happy enough with the status quo, and neither of us were willing to risk the problems that could come with a late pregnancy.

I leaned down and petted my furry child. He opened his mouth in a big grin, and rolled over on his back, waving his legs in the air like a water bug. I got down on the floor and rubbed his belly, as he wanted. I was lucky to have him and Lili in my life. I had my health and a fulfilling career, and the support of caring friends and colleagues. I couldn't ask for more.

As I drove home, the trees along River Road mimicked my mood. The deciduous ones along the riverbank had lost all their leaves, their bare branches skeletons against a looming gray sky. I upped my speed so I could get Rochester walked before the rain came.

As soon as we got to the townhouse, I clipped on his leash and led him out. We walked toward the clubhouse, because there was a big stretch of grass near the entrance that he often liked to utilize.

Earl Garner came down the slight ramp from the entrance to the clubhouse parking lot as we approached. He was wearing a pair of dress slacks and a crew-neck sweater over a button-down shirt, and he had a leather messenger bag slung over the back of his chair.

"Hey, Earl," I said.

"Steve." He nodded. "Rain's coming. Been working in the office getting ready for the new property manager, and now I'm trying to get home before I get soaked."

"Yeah, I'm doing the same thing with Rochester."

He tried to push forward, but Rochester had his nose right up against the leather messenger bag. He swiveled the chair to get the bag away from Rochester, and in the process one of the straps caught in his wheel, and the bag burst open. A thick sheaf of papers fell out and spread over the pavement.

"Here, let me help you with that," I said.

"I can get them," he said angrily.

"Don't be ridiculous, Earl. Let me help." I started picking up the pages before they could blow around in the light wind.

Many of the pages were printouts of email messages to and from Todd Chatzky, with the Pennsylvania Properties logo prominent at the bottom of each message. I picked up one and saw that it was a list of which residents had liens against their property. It looked like Earl had highlighted several of them with a yellow marker.

"Those are not your business!" Early said when he saw me reading.

It began to rain, lightly at first, and then very quickly the rain came down hard and fast. "Screw it," Earl said, and he grabbed the half-open messenger bag and held it on his lap. Then he began wheeling away quickly.

Despite the rain, I picked up every piece of paper I could, holding Rochester's leash in one hand as he strained to go after Earl Garner. By the time I finished I was completely drenched, my hair plastered to my scalp, my T-shirt and shorts clinging to me like a second skin.

Rochester quickly did his business, though he didn't seem to mind the rain, and we hurried home. It was still pouring when we got there, and Rochester stopped underneath the overhang to shake himself.

"Thanks, dog. As if I could get any wetter."

Lili opened the door with a big bath towel in her hands, and I turned Rochester over to her. I stripped naked and left wet footprints all the way to the guest bath, where the washer and drier were. I left the pile of wet paper on the drier, then threw my clothes in the washer and dried myself with a couple of hand towels.

"What happened to you?" Lili asked. She leaned past me and threw the wet bath towel into the washer with my clothes.

I held up the pile of wet paper and explained how it had come from Earl Garner's messenger bag. "You go upstairs, take a shower and dry off," she said. "Leave the papers with me. When I was in Colombia once for a story all the reporter's paper notes got soaked, and we dried them off."

"You're a gem," I said, and I kissed her on the lips. Then my body remembered it was naked, and I grabbed a hand towel, put it over me, and hurried upstairs.

By the time I returned downstairs, Lili had placed a couple of the big coarse bath sheets we used to dry Rochester across the dining room table. Each of the pages from Garner's messenger bag was lined up like a row of soldiers. She was running a hair dryer lightly over pages. "This is going to take a while," she said. "And I'm not sure how much we'll be able to salvage. You should start reading while the ink is still visible, even if it's runny."

Lili had arranged a couple of pages on ivory bond paper at the far end of the table. Those looked like Pennsylvania Properties letterhead, and they were copies of letters that the company president had sent to Earl Garner.

I began reading and making notes. The most recent letter was a direct criticism of Garner's leadership of the board. It pointed out that many of the problems existed because of the policies or lack of enforcement that he and the board had created.

I called Lili over and showed it to her. "This is proof that the people on Hi Neighbor are making valid complaints," I said.

"Down at the other end I saw a sheet with a list of properties with liens against them," she said. "It's hard to read because the yellow highlighter ran in the rain. But you think Earl Garner was taking advantage of people with liens against their properties and buying cheap?"

"I think that's exactly true."

I continued reading, and then I called Rick and asked him to come over and look at what I had assembled. I was worried that Earl Garner would realize that I had those papers, and how incriminating they were, and come after me to retrieve them.

Lili and I used paper towels and the hair dryer to blot the pages, and by the time Rick got there we had arranged the most incriminating evidence at one end of the table.

Lili and I continued to dry as Rick read. "It looks like Earl

Garner's little empire is crashing down around his head," he said, after a while. "Pennsylvania Properties wants to have the whole board removed, and Todd Chatzky assembled this data about Garner taking advantage of people in financial trouble or with big liens against their properties."

"The stuff Todd assembled is dated only two days before his death," I said. "Is it possible that Garner thought he could head off this trouble if he got Todd out of the way?"

"You mean does this give Garner a motive to kill Chatzky? I'd say yes."

"You think the chief will agree?"

"Let's get all this paper dry and organized, and I'll show it to him tomorrow. He'll have to rule on how admissible all this is, considering how you got it."

"When Earl Garner left this stuff on the ground, that's as good as abandoning it, isn't it? So there's no law that says I can't pick up paper from the street."

"It's not that you couldn't pick it up. It's that I—and by extension the police department and the district attorney – only have your word on how you got these. You could have fabricated them yourself."

He held up a hand to forestall any argument. "I know you, and I trust you. At the very least, this ought to be enough to convince the chief to get a search warrant for the original emails and any copies of the written letters."

That would have to be enough.

27: Blocking

We continued to dry and read and organize. The papers that were dated after Todd's death were the most incriminating. The president of Pennsylvania Properties threatened to recommend a new board to pursue a civil suit for breach of fiduciary duty if Garner and the rest of the board did not resign immediately.

It was nearly ten o'clock by the time we were finished, with the damp papers carefully packed between layers of paper towels. He insisted on going out on a quick walk with Rochester and me, just in case Garner was lurking somewhere in the shadows eager for a confrontation.

I didn't believe he'd be out there, but I'd been wrong about that kind of thing in the past, so I was glad Rick was with us.

§ § § §

Saturday morning, the streets of River Bend were still damp from intermittent rain during the night, and the wash of negative ions left a freshness in the air. I was careful to stay away from the twin lakes and the area where Todd had died, and from Earl Garner's street.

After breakfast, I was antsy, waiting to hear from Rick. But I didn't know how easy it would be for him to get hold of the chief on the weekend and I knew I couldn't sit around doing nothing. I decided to take Rochester up to a park along the canal, a few miles north of Stewart's Crossing, where he could run along the towpath and dart in and out of the stand of trees between it and the river.

On our way out of River Bend, I passed the street where Earl Garner lived, and I was surprised to see his wife and son carrying suitcases out of the house and into the Mercedes SUV that Garner drove. Were they running away?

I turned down the next street and circled back, parking in front of a house down the street from Garner's. Then I called Rick. "Garner may be heading out of town," I said. "How quick can you get a reason to stop him?"

"I'm working on it now with the district attorney. I'll send a couple of uniforms over to block them in while I work."

I waited in my parking spot as Garner's wife and son finished packing the SUV. Garner's wife slid into the passenger seat, and Garner pulled his wheelchair up to the driver's side. I watched as he quickly hoisted himself up and into the seat. His son folded the chair and took it around to the back. Then the boy climbed in.

What should I do? Let Garner get on the road and follow him? Or block him in until the police could arrive?

He began to pull the van out, and I put my car in gear and drove right up behind him. I parked on the street, blocking his driveway, and he blew his horn at me.

I didn't do anything, just hunkered down in my seat and waited. After a moment, Mrs. Garner got out of the SUV and came to the passenger side of my car. She saw Rochester there, and then walked around to my side.

I rolled my window down an inch. "You're blocking us in," she said. "We need to get out of our driveway."

"That's pretty evident to me," I said.

"Then why won't you move?"

"Because the police are on their way. Your husband may have killed Todd Chatzky and I'm not going to let him get away with it."

She looked like I had slapped her face. "My husband didn't kill anyone."

"That's for the police and the district attorney, and eventually a judge or a jury to decide," I said. "Right now I'm just a concerned citizen helping the police with their inquiries."

"You're crazy." She turned and strode over to where Earl was leaning out the window of the Mercedes. They started arguing, though I couldn't make out what they were saying.

Then a police car pulled onto the street, and I moved forward, giving the marked car the opportunity to take my space in front of Garner's SUV. I watched as an officer got out and walked up to talk to Garner and his wife.

"I have the search warrant in my hand," Rick said, when I called him. "I'm on my way to River Bend right now."

"You want me to wait here?"

"No. I want you to get out of there and let the police handle this. The officer has explicit instructions not to let Garner leave before I arrive."

I didn't want to leave, but I'd worked enough with Rick to recognize a tone in his voice that needed to be obeyed. I didn't want to go too far away, so I shelved the idea of the towpath park and drove into Stewart's Crossing, where I parked in front of the Chocolate Ear.

I was too wired for coffee, but I could handle a good hot chocolate, and Gail, with her background as a chocolatier, made some wonderfully flavored ones. My mouth was salivating as I parked and led Rochester into the side room where dogs were allowed. I was surprised to see Mark Figueroa and Brody there.

Mark wore jeans and a white cashmere sweater that was almost exactly the color of Brody's coat. Made the problem of dog hair less important, I guessed.

Rochester tugged forward to them, and I heard Mark say, "Brody. Sit," in a commanding voice. Brody sat there as Rochester approached, and the two dogs nuzzled each other. Then Brody rolled onto his belly, and Rochester leaned down to sniff him.

"You think I can leave Rochester here for a minute while I get a hot chocolate?"

"Brody knows that he has to behave in public. I'm sure they'll be okay."

"I'll make it quick." I hurried next door and waited impatiently as Gail brewed a raspberry hot chocolate for me, then decorated it with whipped cream and chocolate curls. Normally I loved standing there, inhaling the scents of chocolate and coffee, relaxing in the casual Parisian atmosphere. But that morning I was too worried about Rochester's behavior, and what was happening at Earl Garner's house.

I resisted the urge to hurry Gail, and then grasped the warm mug gratefully. I walked through the swinging door that separated the food-service part of the café to the dog-friendly room and was surprised to see Rochester and Brody snuggled against each other on the floor. At least one worry was banished.

"How are things going with the house?" I asked Mark, as I slid into the chair across from Mark. He looked more relaxed than he had in a while, and I was glad to see it.

"We got approved for a mortgage on Drew Greenbaum's mom's property yesterday, and we're going to close in the middle of next month," he said.

"That's awesome. How does Joey feel about all this?"

"It's really interesting. We had a long talk at the beginning of the week."

I had heard Joey's end of that story and was interested to hear viewpoint. "And?"

"He is such a guy," Mark said. "I know, that sounds silly. But nobody ever taught him to be open about his feelings. He's had a charmed life, so it never mattered before. But with these problems with his dad, and the new boss at work, he started getting stressed, and he wouldn't tell me what was wrong."

"Excuse me for pointing out the obvious, but you're a guy, too. What makes you different?"

He picked up his coffee, in a white china mug, and sipped. "I had more problems growing up than Joey did. I had a huge growth spurt when I hit puberty, so I was taller than everybody else in my class, and kids used to make fun of me. One guy coined this named for me, the jolly gay giant, complete with the ho-ho-ho."

He pursed his lips, and for a moment it looked like he was blinking back tears. "My grandmother was very sweet, and she encouraged me to tell her when anything was wrong. I got accustomed to talking. Joey never had to learn that skill until now."

"And he has?"

"So far so good. He was worried that I might leave him if he had to do too much for his parents."

I was surprised. "You wouldn't do that."

"I wouldn't. But you know how it is when you get caught up in your own head. We talked it through, and I made him confront his worst fears. His dad dying, his mom getting sick and needing lots of help. I convinced him that we would face anything that happened together."

"That's awesome."

"He's the youngest son, you know, and he was this big baseball star, so everybody babied him and he never had to step up to any responsibility. But now he's changing. He's the one who helped his dad get set up in rehab, and he's already been over at their house rearranging furniture and helping his mom clear out some junk to make it easier for his dad to move around."

"That's good."

"And with buying the house, he's been a great partner, too. We split up the responsibilities – I handle the financial stuff and he's doing all the inspection and renovation plans. I know I can trust him to carry through everything, which is a big relief for me."

He smiled. "Not that I'm saying he's been lazy or anything. Joey's one of the hardest-working guys I know. But it's the taking responsibility part that shows me he's changing."

"I'm glad for you both. And looking forward to having you guys as neighbors. I've got my eye on that back yard of yours as a doggie playground."

"Joey's already a step ahead of you. He's drawing up landscaping plans to make shady places for Brody to rest, and a straight stretch for him to run and chase Frisbees."

We chatted some more as we drank, and the dogs nuzzled each other. Then Mark had to open the antique store. I gave up waiting for Rick to call me, and took Rochester up to the canal park. As he raced around, I kept looking at my phone, hoping Rick would call with information about what was happening with Earl Garner.

I felt bad for Garner's wife and son, to see the police show up to investigate, maybe even to witness Garner being arrested. But that was the way the world worked. People did bad things, and those around them had to suffer, too, even though they weren't at fault.

Had anyone else suffered when I went to prison? I never knew how Mary felt at that time. We had stopped talking to each other after the second miscarriage, and after my arrest, while I waited for my trial, neither of us mentioned the chance that I'd go to prison. She worked with an attorney during that time, though I didn't realize it until she had me served with divorce papers during my first week inside. That showed how deep our lack of communication ran.

I was sure my father had been hurt, too. He never understood exactly what I had done, or why, just that I'd broken the law and had to be punished. I didn't realize it at the time, but he was suffering with his own fatal diagnosis, not wanting to worry me or add extra pressure.

Lack of communication all around. I was glad that Joey and Mark were talking. I had tried to remedy that problem with Lili.

She and I talked about everything, the good and the bad. When we were angry with each other, we explained why, and figured out a common ground, instead of retreating into silence. She knew everything about my job at Friar Lake, my friendships and my occasional forays into hacking.

I knew about her marriages, her divorces, the dangers she had faced as a photojournalist. She shared the joys and frustrations of her teaching and administrative work, and her love for photography. There were things I had yet to learn about her, and that I had yet to tell her about me, but they were minor things that would come up eventually.

Earl Garner and his wife, however, had reached a point when their secrets would become public knowledge, and even if he had murdered a man in cold blood, I felt sorry for him and his family.

28: Two-Headed Wolf

Rick finally called me that evening. The officers had prevented Garner and his family from leaving while they searched the house and the van. They found Garner's knife, which matched the kind of blade used to kill Todd Chatzky, and independently located evidence that showed Garner and his board had abused their fiduciary duties at River Bend.

Rick had compared the wheels on Garner's chair to the marks on the pavement near where Todd's body had been found, and they matched. He had spoken with Oscar Panaccio, who confirmed that he had seen Todd leave the clubhouse on foot, and that Garner had followed in his wheelchair.

It was still a lot of circumstantial evidence, but it was enough to arrest Garner for the murder of Todd Chatzky. Garner hadn't said a word, and had immediately invoked his right to counsel, calling in a Temple law classmate who specialized in criminal defense.

"He's going to be a hard nut to crack," Rick said. "I doubt he will admit to anything, which means I'm going to have to work even harder to prove what he did."

"If I can help you with anything, let me know."

"I will. Right now it's just a matter of solid policework."

Within a week, we received a certified letter from Pennsylvania Properties that because of financial improprieties, the board of directors of River Bend had been dismissed. The new property manager would handle all decisions until a new board could be elected and impaneled.

One evening soon after we got the letter from the management company, I was at dinner with Lili and said, "I was thinking. I'd like to have this house retitled in both our names."

She looked up at me. "Really?"

"Why not? I want you to be protected in case anything happens to me. If you're on the deed as a joint tenant with right of survivorship, the house goes directly to you, without probate. You're already on my pension and the one who inherits all my investments."

"You want me to run for the board, don't you?"

I smiled. "You're always one step ahead of me, sweetheart. But yes, if you're an owner, you're eligible to run for the board, and I think you'd do a terrific job. Is that something you want?"

"I think so. I want to do my part to bring the property values back up and to make this a safe, happy place for us to live."

The message boards on Hi Neighbor began buzzing with posts about Todd's death and Earl Garner's arrest, and suggestions for new board members. The management company discovered that the board had squirreled away money to pay for road repairs but never hired a company to do the work, so they did, and one evening, as I was walking Rochester, the smell of hot tar floated in the late autumn air.

Ahead of us, I saw Epiphania Kosta. She had her older son by the hand, and the younger one was in a pouch on the chest of the man with her. "Steve, this is my husband Nick," she said. "I told him about what a great job you did for the League at Friar Lake."

We shook hands, which was kind of awkward with the baby between us. "I work for Polymathia University – we're a user-friendly mostly online operation, but some of our degrees require occasional in-person sessions."

I wondered if the choice of a Greek name meant it was Nick's company, and asked.

"Nope, I'm just the vice president for facility management. We're making a name for ourselves in the for-profit college zone because we vet our candidates very thoroughly, and encourage them to use scholarships and grants to fund their education rather than taking out big loans."

Interesting, but I'd have to research Polymathia online and make sure they were as honest as Nick Kosta said.

"We have been hosting occasional in-person sessions at St. Barnabas College in Philadelphia, but they're shutting down and selling the property to a real estate developer. Do you think we could use Friar Lake?"

"What would you need?"

The baby kicked him in the stomach as we talked, and we agreed that he would email me a list of his requirements, and I'd see what I could do. As we said goodbye, I heard the landscape company working on the hedges down the street from us. The management had been reprimanded, and our hedges were now neatly trimmed, the yards mowed and edged. A couple of broken light fixtures had been replaced and the brick pavers at a couple of intersections repaired, along with the piece of sidewalk where Sylvia Greenbaum had fallen.

The next morning I researched Polymathia, and then checked with President Babson. I was worried that he wouldn't approve of connecting Eastern with a competitor, but he reassured me he was happy to support education—and bring in revenue whenever he could.

Over a period of weeks, Nick Kosta and I negotiated a plan for the winter term. An executive MBA program would meet for a total of eight three-day weekends at Friar Lake, while the low-residency MFA program in creative writing would take over the facility for two weeks in mid-May. The revenue from those programs gave me a comfortable cushion against any cost-cutting efforts from the administration and secured my job for the next year at least.

Within a month of Todd Chatzky's death cold weather had us firmly in its grip. It was hard to judge the job the landscapers were doing, because all the leaves had fallen and been blown away, and hedges and lawns were in hibernation. It would take until the first snowfall to see if they kept up the improvement in their performance.

One morning in early December I sat down with Joey to go over our plans for the winter break. The last day of class was the eighth of December, with a week of final exams. Grades were due in the college mainframe a day after that, and then the college shut down until the first week of January.

Though Joey and I were both on vacation, we set up a schedule so that one of us visited Friar Lake each week the facility was shut down to make sure no pipes burst or windows shattered while we were gone.

I was pleased to see that Joey had returned to his cheerful, happy-go-lucky self. "Any plans for the break?" I asked.

"Work on the house," he said. "My dad got out of rehab last week, and he's going to come over and supervise me, hold the ladder for me and that kind of thing."

"Have you heard anything about Sylvia Greenbaum?"

"I spoke to Drew last week. He's got her in a good quality memory care facility near where he lives in Virginia, and he's getting his real estate license so he can have a flexible schedule to check in with her."

"That's great."

Joey leaned back, stretching his long legs out beside Rochester. "How about you?"

"I think I might be able to relax," I said. "I found someone else to take over the financial planning programs for the professor on sabbatical and booked a couple of other small meetings for January and February. With the revenue from Polymathia University I'll be able to exceed all my goals for the winter term. That means I can chill, read, play with Rochester and hang out with Lili."

I got a different opinion of life with Joey and Mark when I ran into Mark at The Chocolate Ear a couple of days later. Our coffee maker had broken, and while I waited for the Amazon elves to ship me a new one I dropped into Gail's on the way to work with Rochester by my side. He was happy to get a biscuit there, and I wondered if secretly he had planned to sabotage the coffee maker for just that reason.

Sometimes, you don't know with dogs.

"How come you're here, and not home preparing for your open house this weekend?" I asked Mark. Brody wasn't with him, but Rochester greeted him effusively nonetheless.

"Because my father-in-law is there, and the two-headed wolf scares me." Mark had always joked that Joey's last name meant "head of the wolf" in Italian, and that when he and his father got together they were so similar that it was like having a two-headed wolf around.

"Come on, Joe Senior isn't that bad. And he and Joey's mom love you."

"They do, and I'm very grateful for that, believe me. But Joe Senior has an opinion on every tool Joey uses, every way he turns the wrench. He criticizes the way Joey holds a hammer as if he was a golf pro analyzing a swing."

"And Joey puts up with that?"

"He says that he almost lost his dad, so he's willing to tolerate some irritation. Which, by the way, is a major change. Six months ago Joey would have politely escorted his dad out of the house and double-locked the door behind him."

"Ah, for that happy-go-lucky boy you fell in love with," I said.

"He's still around." Mark smiled. "Just not twenty-four-seven."

"And that, my friend, is the issue with growing up," I said.

I drove up to Friar Lake with Rochester by my side, the heat on in the car but the passenger window cracked enough that he could stick his snout out of it. That morning I heard from Rick. Earl Garner still hadn't said a word about Todd's death, but enough circumstantial evidence had been accumulated, and Earl's old law-school pal had convinced him to take a plea deal rather than stand trial for murder. As part of that, Pennsylvania Properties agreed not to push forward complaints against Garner or any of the other board members for lack of fiduciary responsibility.

Garner's home was on the market, and I had a small sense of satisfaction that property values had not bounced up yet, so he was likely to take a loss. The more important loss, though, would be the one Garner's son felt when his father was in prison. I had seen them playing ball together, felt the connection between them, and now that would be gone.

Saturday evening, we brought Rochester over to Joey and Mark's new house for the big party. They had already made friends with many of the dog owners and canines in the community, so when we got there, Brody was in the chilly back yard romping with Gargamel the English Setter and Angel the white Coton de Tulear. I sent Rochester out there to play with his friends.

It was a warm, happy evening, and I was glad that Joey and Mark were settling easily into River Bend, and that Joe Senior had recovered from his heart attack. I wished him well, though I didn't add that I hoped the two-headed wolf would continue to thrive.

I gave a toast later, in which I welcomed Joey, Mark and Brody, and said that I hoped our neighborhood would be well-kept and happy for a long time to come. Outside, the wind shook the branches of the pines and Norway spruce, the gibbous moon shone a path to the doorway, and a pair of squirrels paused in the newly paved street, then romped together up into the trees.

Thanks for reading about Steve and Rochester! *Dog's Green Earth* is the tenth in the series—have you read them all?

THE SERIES IN ORDER

In Dog We Trust

The Kingdom of Dog

Dog Helps Those

Dog Bless You

Whom Dog Hath Joined

Dog Have Mercy

Honest to Dog

Dog is in the Details

Dog Knows

Dog's Green Earth

If you're a Kindle Unlimited reader, you'll find omnibus volumes of books 1-3 (Three Dogs in a Row) and books 4-6 (Three More Dogs in a Row).

Author's Note

Rick's four motives for murder, love, lust, lucre and loathing, come from a quote by P.D. James. But since he's a cop rather than a reader, he doesn't realize that.

This book is for Brody and Griffin, and for their daddy.

"Put me anywhere on God's green earth, I'll triple my worth."
Jay-Z, "U Don't Know"

About the Author

Neil Plakcy's golden retriever mysteries are inspired by his own golden, Samwise, who was just as sweet as Rochester, though not quite as smart. And fortunately he didn't have Rochester's talent for finding dead bodies. Now that Sam has gone on to his big, comfy bed in heaven, his place by Neil's side has been taken by Brody and Griffin, a pair of English Cream goldens with a penchant for mischief.

A native of Bucks County, PA, where the golden retriever mysteries are set, Neil is a graduate of the University of Pennsylvania, Columbia University and Florida International University, where he received his MFA in creative writing. A professor of English at Broward College's South Campus, he has written and edited many other books; details can be found at his website, http://www.mahubooks.com. He is also past president of the Florida chapter of Mystery Writers of America.

Made in the USA
San Bernardino, CA
01 November 2019